EMPIRE

Mary O'Donnell

EMPIRE

ARLEN
HOUSE

Empire

is published in 2018 by
ARLEN HOUSE
42 Grange Abbey Road
Baldoyle
Dublin 13
Ireland
Phone: 353 86 8360236
Email: arlenhouse@gmail.com
arlenhouse.blogspot.com

Distributed internationally by
SYRACUSE UNIVERSITY PRESS
621 Skytop Road, Suite 110
Syracuse, NY 13244–5290
Phone: 315–443–5534/Fax: 315–443–5545
Email: supress@syr.edu

978–1–85132–175–9, paperback

Typesetting by Arlen House

CONTENTS

EMPIRE

I

Dublin

Margaret wanted to dash off one last letter to Mother before they departed, but William said there would not be time. He was with the porters, pointing at several trunks and six smaller suitcases outside Westland Row Station.

But surely there was time for a last postcard, she pressed; she could write it rapidly and have it posted while he dealt with the luggage. William threw her a look, his normally cheerful eyes losing their colour as his mood frayed. In the end, she adjusted her new blue hat and said nothing. She would handle the matter herself.

Before he could object, she mounted the steps to the station, enjoying the swirl of cooling air that blew from the train tracks on the humid autumn afternoon, and hurried to the newsagents. The man behind the counter smiled as she approached. Laden with small packages from the Grafton Street shops, she used often buy a quarter of powdered bonbons or a newspaper. The fellow raised his hat to her now, a small brown bowler perched like an egg with a rim on what she imagined was a balding head.

'One plain postcard please,' she said breathlessly.

'Of course, Mrs Wheeler. A postage stamp perhaps?'

'Thank you,' she replied, opening her purse and counting coins.

She glanced up questioningly.

'Threepence farthing.' He sighed, apparently at the cost, but said nothing.

She handed him the coins, snapped shut the metal clasp on her purse, enjoying the rather important sound it made, then took both postcard and stamp. She licked the stamp and fixed it to the card, before turning to leave.

'Good day to you, Mrs Wheeler.'

'Goodbye, Mr Murphy,' she replied as she glanced back, then hurried to her left to sit on a bench in the main station and scribble a final note to Mother. With luck, she would receive it in the afternoon. To her dismay, she was perspiring, but temperatures were above normal for the time of year. That, and the strain of departure, as well as weeks of listening to William and his infernal organising, was surely contributing to her heated state. The prospect of going to Burma had bothered her for months now, so that every morning on awakening, she had experienced a fearful pain in her stomach.

Around her, people moved rapidly. The Wexford train was in, and a long line of passengers had disembarked to make their way in clusters up the platform. Her eye swept over them automatically, observing hats with velvet trims, pin-tucks and faggoting on the dresses of some of the ladies. Then she bent her head and concentrated:

Dearest Mother,
I write in haste as we have but moments before boarding the train.
As I said this morning, I will write tomorrow from England, and by
the time we reach Southampton I will have something more to say
than this feeble adieu. All will be well, so you must not worry, and

as we have so often said, dear Francis will take care of you and be the attentive son you know him to be, despite the worry of his rebellious ideas.
With utmost love,
your affectionate daughter,
Margaret.
P.S. I have packed the gong most carefully in the new mahogany trunk! It will arrive in excellent condition, so have no concern about that. I shall have our servant use it to announce our meals.

Her fine fingers sealed the card, then she made her way across the tiled waiting area to the postbox. Now, to face William. Despite herself, she smiled at the thought of Mother's gong, the one domestic keepsake from the home she had grown up in, on Sydney Parade. It was the only thing she fancied, what Mother called 'a trifle', knowing how greatly she liked it, insisting Margaret take it on the journey overseas. It will be put to good use in your new home, Mother had said, a little more gravely than Margaret would have liked.

At the thoughts of the gong, she felt slightly more cheerful, and hurried back down the steps and onto the street. The trunks and cases had been emptied from the automobile, and William was passing something – money, she presumed – to the driver. It could all have been so much worse, she thought, had they had children. But thankfully, that was not yet the case, although of late she had been feeling so peculiar that she wondered if she were not already 'expecting'. There had been no time, in the end, to visit Dr Armstrong, who lived around the corner from their home on Herbert Place, so she had tried to put the matter out of her mind and hope for the best.

She knew that already she was grieving for her home, for the loss for a long time to come, of the adorable, elegant house in which they had happily settled a mere two years before. As an engineer William was now in great demand, which was the reason they were leaving for Burma. That, and his restlessness. Somehow, Dublin was too small for him, although he had grown up in Rathgar, which, quiet village though it was, was still within reach of everything the marvellous city had to offer.

It would be a splendid new venture, he had told her practically every day once the idea arose. Thanks to the Suez Canal, they wouldn't even have to travel down the enormous length of Africa and around the Cape, as his uncle Albert had once had to do. He never observed her doubts, or, if he did, he ignored them. In the end, all was agreed before she could register serious objections, and, before she knew it, the passage was booked. First, the boat from Kingstown to Holyhead, then a train to London and onwards to Southampton, from where they would board the ship that would take them through some of the world's hottest regions, until they docked at Rangoon. Nor would it end there. What would follow was an almighty train journey to Mandalay, right in the mysterious heart of that rich country, close to the tribesmen whom the British had been organising since the early nineteenth century. There were roads to be built and bridges to be constructed in snake-infested territory with few doctors and even fewer hospitals.

They would have a marvellous home, William had assured her, with vastly more rooms than at Herbert Place, and a nanny, should they require one. At this, he had winked at her and grinned sheepishly. There would also be a cook and a servant or two. She would have no need for that silly little gong, he had teased. Out there, monks struck gigantic copper ones in monasteries and palaces, which echoed throughout the royal city, into the big teak wood houses, and out into the surrounding jungle. But Margaret did not care about a struck gong in some pagoda or monastery, and reminded William that it was for their domestic pleasure. As if to appease her, and although it was not quite relevant, he added that she would have the advantage of the companionship of other, like-minded women. Although Margaret very much doubted that she would meet another like-minded woman in Mandalay, she kept this thought to herself.

'Margaret Ward! My sweet, we must hurry,' William announced roguishly gripping her elbow and addressing her by her family name as he steered her towards the station steps.

'The train isn't letting people on yet,' she murmured, shaking him off.

'No matter. Always good to be on time, eh?'

As ever, they were too early. Margaret persuaded him to go to the tearooms because it would be a good half hour before the train for Kingstown Pier arrived.

In the end, though, they had barely ordered a pot of tea from a young country waitress, when it arrived, and once again William hustled her along.

'Not so fast, William, not so fast!' she said impatiently. She was breathless. Once again he had her by the elbow, ushering her as if she were a piece of stolen goods, or some object he could not wait to get out of Dublin – no, out of the country, she thought with irritation.

Once they were on the train, she managed to calm herself. It was going to be a spectacular journey and she was very fortunate to have this opportunity. Mother was wrong. William was right. He sometimes was, and despite misgivings she would try to trust his judgement.

Kingstown was humming with turmoil. She boarded the ship before William, who entrusted her with her ticket while he checked that everything was in order and their luggage was not misplaced – though how he would do that was a conundrum, given the number of other travellers, which included the casual labourers crossing over to find work in England. She watched as they too boarded, with shabby coats and worn caps, clutching small packages and simple valises. Nobody could blame the men and women who left the slums. She knew from Mother, who was a regular visitor to the women lying-in, how babies and even new mothers often died within months of a birth. And the men had no work, as Francis was always saying.

Mother had initially frowned on the idea of organised labourers, but slightly over two years earlier, the debacle on Sackville Street had convinced her that the men had no choice but to fight, when they were locked out of their jobs because they refused to pledge never to join the union. She had since commented that some people had no knowledge of how hard the lives of other Dubliners were. And if Father had not left her in such comfort on his death, who knew where they all might be? This rhetorical question was put to both Margaret and Francis by Mrs Ward with monotonous regularity, so much so that both brother and sister came to resent it. After all, they were not responsible for the fact that they had been born into a household of some comfort, any more than they were responsible for the premature death of Father, in middle age, from a heart attack.

From the ship's rail, she kept her eye on William as he moved through the crowds weaving past women in shawls, clusters of children, past a paper boy calling out the day's headline, until he made his way to speak to some official in charge of loading up the bulky luggage from the Dublin train. She smiled. Dear William, she thought charitably – how busy he loved to be.

As she looked down, watching William's slightly unruly brown head of hair, thoughts of many important events flickered through her mind. Father's death seemed so long ago. At ten years' remove, it was a very different country to peer back into. How on earth would she – or any of them – manage to explain to him how the world had changed since 1905?

He had missed the Great Exhibition in Herbert Park, only two years after his death. The three of them – Mother,

Francis and she – had passed the day so pleasurably and stylishly, it still thrilled Margaret to think about it. It was so very modern, with many industrial advancements. The adults were quite sedate, as usual, but children and young people were jolly. In the Canadian Water Chute she and Francis had screamed with delight as their boat splashed down from the chute and passed beneath two bridges, before sailing around a small island.

Later on, Father also missed the unimaginable, the thing which had shocked everybody, after which they knew that they were living in a modern, often terrifying world, in which hope could be completely destroyed. She thought of the deaths of people just like her, and of people in the steerage class, and the hundreds from all over Europe, the dismal terror of their drowning in the frozen North Atlantic on that Leviathan of a ship which was supposed to be unsinkable. She glanced around nervously, then shivered, as thoughts of the unknown but imagined rose to torment her, although Kingstown was bathed in late afternoon, golden light.

Father had missed the Lockout in 1913 as well. She very much doubted he would have cared for what happened, especially the rioting and beatings in the streets. There were even shootings, and the Constabulary had disgraced itself among the people.

And now Father was missing the war in Flanders and France, where many of their own – though not Francis – were valiantly fighting the German enemy. No, it would have been impossible to explain to a dead person who had suddenly returned to earth all that they had missed and all that they would now have to become accustomed to. It would be like explaining a whole new country, with a whole new language, to a befuddled stranger.

An hour and a half later, the steam packet set sail. William and Margaret watched as the boat pulled back, at first slowly, gradually turning around within the harbour before moving off with greater speed, the tangible bulk of one of mankind's greatest mechanical works, apart from the automobile.

The October evening had drawn in, gas lights glowed on the streets, and she watched as the small seaside town retracted. Was it running away from them or were they running away from it? It seemed as if they were retreating with greater speed than Kingstown was, as if the ship and its passengers, with their hopes and dreams, could scarcely wait to be shot of Ireland and its flickering lighthouses. She watched as even they faded, Howth, Baily, and finally Kish.

She did not want to be shot of Ireland, of course. Francis certainly disapproved of their going so far away, but that was because, as a good brother, he appreciated her desire to remain in Dublin. She knew, though, that his feeling was also connected to his involvement with the Irish Citizen Army. Francis believed that Irish people should live and work in and for Ireland. He could not, for the life of him, comprehend why William had felt it so critical to bring his engineering skills to Burma, to work under the British. It was not Burma Francis objected to, but the British.

'We still haven't got rid of them ourselves. Can you imagine how those poor people in Burma must be feeling?'

Margaret had not considered the question of Burmese sensibility, but replied that it was only a three year contract. They would be back to Dublin by late 1918, she insisted, where they would then resume their places in society and rear healthy children to whom he, Francis, would be uncle. Francis grunted, as if this was not a realistic way of thinking. He lit a cigarette.

'Want one?' she remembered him asking, as if he had finally given up on the subject.

'Please. I've grown rather fond of them, thanks to William.'

'He doesn't object?'

Margaret laughed. 'Surprisingly no. He says he enjoys watching me smoke.'

'How bizarre.'

'Isn't it just.'

She did not smoke on the towering steamer that left Southampton two days later. She did not dare. Unlike the calm waters of Kingstown Harbour, and the brilliant blackness of the Irish Sea, which had flashed occasionally with broken moonlight on their first night, the southwards tracking along the French coast was ghastly. A dense storm blew from the Atlantic and the ship lunged uneasily forward. Through the porthole of their cabin, the sky was leaden, interspersed occasionally with vicious cracks of lightning that ripped down to the horizon in horrible fingers.

As she emerged for the third time from the closet, William patted the bed on which he was stretched, inviting her to join him.

'You should simply lie down and do nothing until you get your sea legs,' he advised languidly

'Yes dear, but I don't think – I don't think I'm –'

She swallowed and touched her throat to halt the flow of bile that rose again in her gorge, then disappeared back inside the closet. As she leaned over the vile little bowl and emptied what remained of her stomach yet again, the back of her throat stinging, there was a gentle knocking on the narrow door. She reached out and grasped a thin hand towel, wiped her mouth and patted the perspiration off her forehead.

'What?' she groaned.

'You feeling awfully bad?'

At this first sign of sympathy, tears welled in her eyes. Still, she did not open the door.

'Yes.' She struggled to keep her voice steady.

'Shall I call someone? The doctor?'

'I don't think I need a doctor.'

'Shall I order weak tea perhaps?'

'No!'

Again, she leaned over the bowl and retched, then watched a thin stream of watery liquid yet again trail from her mouth. All she wanted was to feel well and healthy. Nothing more, nothing less. She did not want Dublin or Ireland or Burma, she did not want Mother or Francis, nor even William, and Father was too long dead to be of any use. All she wanted was oneness with herself, never mind with the rest of humanity, at least the unsuffering part of humanity on their godforsaken planet. For it was godforsaken, she thought with appalling clarity as her stomach heaved again, or else she would have had some guidance in several matters, instead of which she had allowed herself to drift towards decisions, which – she knew for certain – were not the wisest or most prudent for a young woman of her disposition and intelligence. Why, for example, had she not pressed Mother to allow her to attend University College to study something – anything – that would carry her through her life? English or French, she thought, might have suited her.

She pulled open the door and re-entered the cabin. William was still perched on the bed, shoes kicked off, his shirt draped over her valise. Two buttons on his vest were undone, and he was in the process of removing his crocodile-leather belt.

'It's easy to speak of sea legs, William,' she grumbled. 'And I will lie down. But I have never before been in the condition I now believe I'm in.'

He cocked his left eyebrow.

'God in heaven, you don't think it's TB, do you?'

He jumped to his feet and stared into her face. 'You have been rather flushed lately, haven't you? And that cough last month?'

'No William, I have *not* contracted tuberculosis!'

'But your mother's hospital visits – those lying-in establishments attract all sorts. She might have carried something –'

Before she could stop herself, Margaret pushed him so roughly, he fell back on the bed. It was all she could do not to jump on her husband and pummel him with her fists. Instead, she stood and trembled, atears spurting from her eyes.

'You insult Mother so casually,' she sobbed, more homesick than she could ever have imagined.

He twisted his body to one side, sprang to his feet again, and grasped her tightly by the shoulders.

'How dare you!' She saw that he too was trembling. 'How dare you push me!' Then, evenly, 'I am your husband and you shall honour me. That is what wives do.'

She did not resist him as he gripped her, but she did not weaken either. With this sudden need for concentration, the nausea retreated, even as the ship ploughed on, rising and dipping, even as they staggered from side to side, holding their balance. He continued to grip her, eyes blazing with indignation, his fingers pressed into the firm flesh of her upper arms.

'It is not what wives do entirely,' she replied then, holding his gaze.

'It is what you promised.'

'As did you, William, if you remember.'

He looked puzzled.

'You promised to honour me. Instead you are dragging me to a place I never wanted to go to, a life that frightens me. Honour?' Her eyes blazed. 'Perhaps honour is merely a word.'

At this, he released her, then turned his back, pushing both hands deeper in his trouser pockets.

She would not tell him just then what the rest of her thoughts were. It was too late for some things. She could no longer pretend she was not carrying his child, that these were the early stages of the pregnancy. All she had to do was decide what was in her best interest: to tell him immediately and hope that it would restore a modicum of civility between them for the rest of the voyage. Or not to tell him at all, to disembark in Rome, or Piraeus or whatever damn place the floating metal can she was trapped in might dock for a day. How she hated him at this moment! She would then make her way home, but not before retrieving her gong, the precious gong from the hallway at Herbert Place, and bringing it back to Dublin.

But in a flash, awful as the lightning that tore at the sea outside, she saw her situation and how helpless she was. With not a penny in her pocket beyond the price of a few fripperies, a novel or two to pass the time from the ship's shop, with no really valuable jewellery either, merely a three-stone diamond engagement ring, and Mother's peridot earrings – she could do nothing. So it did not matter at which city she disembarked, because she could not do so and contrive a plan that would see her safely home again.

'I am pregnant.'

He turned and took a step towards her. She watched, almost disappointed at the predictability of it, as his face softened, as his eyes travelled over her face, and along her neck, down over her tender breasts, lower still until they were staring right at her hard belly.

'No wonder you've been out of sorts,' he whispered. 'Your mood – it hasn't been quite – well, no matter, sit down, sit down and rest. You mustn't lift a finger for the remainder of the voyage.'

He meant well. She knew that. He had decided – or rather, his nature had decided – to treat her kindly now that she was carrying his child. She would want for nothing on the trip. He would bother her no more with his hurrying and fussing. This child was something he had always imagined. He would care for her now. She thought miserably of the birth as he settled her on the bed and began to whisper again about ordering tea and a ginger biscuit to settle her stomach. It would be in the mad heat of May, in Burma, and as her belly contracted in agonising pains she would be able to hear the sound of a gigantic gong in some damn monastery.

But she could not think about that just now. If she thought ahead to Rangoon, and then the train to Mandalay, she might jump overboard, and her body, with its tiny half-made baby, would then be swept into the Bay of Biscay. While William patted her and murmured, she began to think of the letters she would write home, daily, one to Francis and one to Mother. She would speak to both about what was happening, she would ask Mother for advice while imploring her not to worry.

She would find direction. It was within her power to teach William a thing or two, and in a discreet way that would make their marriage more than tolerable. After all, she was not in her current state because she had been reluctant or shy. He had never forced himself on her. On the contrary, she and William had had the happiest of private moments once an overlong honeymoon in the dripping, cloud-ridden Lake District ended and they established themselves at Herbert Place. What he failed to do in his discourses with her, or when Mother or Francis were present, rolling so many modern ideas around their new home that he simply went silent, he sometimes compensated for in other ways. At such moments, his arms around her, he would whisper all kinds of incoherent silliness in her ear, quite unlike the daytime William who held his dignity. He would pour words and ardour down along her neck, her breasts, her belly. Mother had once warned that, in marriage, things might be different from what she expected, but Margaret did not think that this was quite what Mother intended. She had not been suggesting pleasant surprises so much as a note of caution. She had meant well, just as William was now meaning well.

Sexual congress – a stupid phrase she had once heard a Redemptorist priest utter at a packed women's evening in Rathmines Church – was all very well, and the priest said it might bring grace to some marriages, but it was not everything. He was entirely incorrect, she knew. Sexual congress meant a great deal when the man and woman admired one another. However, William would have to be decent to her at all times, because thoughtlessly, he viewed her as a vessel on which he could set sail, as if she were the steamship that was carrying them now towards Rangoon, nautical mile by nautical mile.

He buttoned up his shirt, pulled on his jacket, then moved towards the cabin door before turning back towards her. He was smiling, and very charmingly. 'I'm going to order sweet tea for you, my dear, and some dry biscuits. And a stiff whiskey for me!'

He was gone in a flash. She unbuttoned her boots, hitched her dress up around her knees and lay back on the bed. It was almost comfortable. The ship droned on through the night, nosing and dipping, rising and dropping. But her stomach had settled and she felt steadier than she had done for some time. William had said there would be a nanny in Mandalay. She would have plenty of help to assist her with a baby. In the scented, teak-ceilinged rooms she imagined their home to possess, near the jungle, where banana leaves flapped noisily in monsoon breezes, there would eventually be a child with buttery curls and pale skin.

2

Mandalay

In May, Margaret gave birth after ten hours during which she thought she would die, in which she was occasionally very frightened, believing herself incapable of pushing a baby from her body. In the teak-walled bedroom of their house in Mandalay, with its mosquito drapes all around her, she was attended by her maid Kyi, and a vague-sounding, over-deferential Indian doctor who seemed terrified of laying a hand on her throughout the ordeal. But in the end a beautiful baby boy emerged from her body, slippery and scented with birth. Immediately, she clasped the child to her chest, and nuzzled it with her cheek, awed by a softness and sweetness she had never, in her wildest dreams, imagined to be possible in any human encounter.

During those months, settling into their house on Orchid Road had not been easy. At first, she believed the vituperative heat would eventually beat her, and that she would be forced to return to Ireland with Henry, as they named their son, regardless of William's contract. As she recovered her energies, she stayed indoors for much of the day, unable to tolerate the unremitting blue skies that sat like great molten plates, quietly aghast that such heat burned for thousands of miles throughout the Orient, that there was no reprieve, and no coolness to be found, save for walking at dawn before the first blades of sunlight struck the trees, or else lying in baths of tepid water. But she could not pass her existence in a bath of tepid water, and Kyi must regard her as very strange indeed. Although Kyi understood English, she did not speak it easily, and instead frequently murmured to her in her own tongue. Whether this was a reply or a question, Margaret never knew, but it was not problematic. Kyi's family home was a mile away, a low-lying timber shack which accommodated Kyi, her husband and his mother. Her only child had died,

Margaret gleaned, but how exactly this had happened remained unclear to her.

Sometimes, she regarded the little gong which had been so carefully packed and included in their luggage for the long voyage. It stood rather uselessly now in the large timbered hallway which led through to the living quarters, its polish long dulled from the humidity and an absence of brass polish. Kyi struggled to keep the brass gleaming and golden, so great was the humidity and heat, and on the one occasion Margaret had asked cook to strike the gong to announce dinner, they could scarcely hear more than a thin high quavering sound. So ineffective was it in the wide space of their home, with the dining room situated at the opposite end of the house, that it suddenly lost all meaning, and now sat insignificantly swamped by the intense energies, metals and temperatures that were gradually rearranging Margaret's life.

One year after her son's birth, she found herself pregnant again.

'Henry certainly needs a little brother,' William said cheerfully one morning as he shaved himself.

'Or a little sister would also suffice.'

He said nothing, convinced as he was that two children might not be enough, if the second one were female.

On this matter Margaret had made up her mind however. Towards the middle of the second pregnancy, William was struck down with malaria, and she had to care for him in his weakness. This was after his third trip to Pyawadi, where the Eastwood Construction Company suspension bridge project was moving ahead with some urgency. The way through the teak forest had been cleared, lumber removed by teams of elephants towards the river, and the building site for the new bridge was being made ready. As she watched over William during this period, never certain whether he would live or die, she resolved that there would not be a third confinement. It was not because she had not generally enjoyed the experience of being a mother. She had, in fact, begun to feel quite strong despite the heat, especially once she stopped breast-feeding the ravenous Henry and handed him over to Kyi's gentle care. But in the middle of her second pregnancy, moving cumbrously, she knew that if at all possible, there would not be a third child born to the Wheeler household, whether in Burma or Ireland. Well aware that preventatives of many kinds existed, she did not have any in her possession, nor was it likely that she would come by any before their return home when William's contract expired. She would just have to be careful. They would devise other ways of pleasuring one another when they felt in the mood for love. It had never been beyond their imaginations before, so why should it now be any different?

Yet she wished she had spoken more frankly to Mother prior to their departure, because Mother, she knew, was knowledgeable about matters pertaining to women's freedom. She was also curious about an item she had mentioned in a private letter to her, which she had ordered from London. The Violet Wand, as it was called, soothed all rheumatic pain, Mrs Ward assured her, and apparently in the most delightful manner. But it was definitely not a preventative, and therefore of no immediate use to Margaret, even if one had been available to her.

When he was at his most delirious, William saw snakes everywhere. It coincided with the monsoon season, and even when Margaret and Kyi were bending over him solicitously, there was no convincing him that the room was not beset by green pythons, one thicker and longer than another. He would cry out in terror, shielding his face and clinging to his own throat as the spectres writhed and invaded. There was little to do, the doctor had advised, but sit it out, keep William cool, and as far as possible, calm.

Gradually, his strength returned, and the pattern of fevers subsided, the drenching night sweats, the intense chills. Instead of slithering, darting snakes came the sound of pariah curs, baying and howling at the full moon. He hated the beasts, although he was a dog lover, but their impassioned racket kept him from sleep and reminded him of old stories from Ireland about banshees and ghostly hounds on shadowy bog roads.

One morning, although still confined to the bedroom, William woke feeling unusually refreshed, and called for Minh, the local man who had accompanied him for weeks on end through the jungle.

'Minh is not here. He left an hour ago for Pyawadi,' Margaret told him. 'Palmer sent a man down. It appears Minh is in favour.'

William grunted at this, taking a sup of smoky black Burmese tea. He swallowed it, then sat back. It wasn't like Palmer, the project supervisor, to favour any of the men who worked on the team. He had probably sent for him out of spite, because he knew he was William's man, and because of what had happened a month ago in Pyawadi.

'I thought I told Kyi to add a little *oolong* when she's brewing tea,' he said testily.

Margaret faced him, hands on hips. 'You know very well that *oolong* varies in quality. If we don't have it, it's because Kyi has decided the quality is poor at the moment. You will just have to accept that and stop behaving like a spoiled boy.'

He said nothing for a moment, then smiled faintly. 'You rely too much on Kyi,' he said softly, before sipping once more at the dark, coffee-coloured brew.

'I could not have survived without her, my dear, and that is the truth, no more than you could have survived this far without Minh.'

Slowly, she set to tidying the room, plumping the bolster that lay along a chartreuse-green silk day-bed that showed signs of mildew. She approached the screened teak windows, shaking the thin muslin curtains, and finally, holding her breath carefully, removed William's chamberpot from beneath the canopied bed with its mosquito netting. He pulled back the netting slightly to watch her, admiring her full belly and the way the fine cream silk of her dress was now stretched tightly beneath her engorged bosom. Despite small dissatisfactions and annoyances, despite the resentments he harboured towards Palmer, he still considered himself a fortunate man. His wife, he had occasionally admitted to himself, usually when slightly drunk, in camp up-country, and bored by the companionship of other men, was the true beginning and end of his existence, once work was done. And what else did he work for, but to provide her, and them both, and the long line of children he hoped they might have together, with comfort, opportunity and the prospect of progress? He continually reminded himself of this, especially in the wake of the last trip to Pyawadi, which was also when he had contracted malaria.

'I will call in on you at eleven o'clock,' Margaret said, 'with a cup of Mother's Malted Milk. It arrived yesterday and will build you up. Try to rest until then.'

'But what about Minh? I need to speak to him.'

'I'll dispatch one of the men. Perhaps he will return.'

William hesitated. 'No – don't send anyone. It will annoy Palmer if Minh doesn't show up at camp, and he'll only punish him later for disobedience or recalcitrance or whatever excuse he can concoct against him.'

'But he's *your* man!'

'Palmer's word goes. I won't risk anything happening to Minh.'

Before she left the room, holding the chamberpot at arm's length, she smiled cheerfully back at him. 'We are lucky, aren't we, to have both found a local person with whom we have some kind of sympathy?'

Sometimes, Margaret felt quite satisfied with her own progress. In Burma, despite its difficulties, she had become a real wife and mother. The days of being a honeymooning flibbertijibbet were long behind her, she knew. She had learned how to speak back to William when he became fussy and peremptory; indeed, if anything – she smiled at the thought, she herself had become a little high-handed with *him* when called for. There was no doubt about it, the Margaret Ward whom William had courted only a few years before, had evolved into a Mrs Margaret Wheeler who had, in the course of that time, acquired a great deal of self-knowledge. The only pity was, she had so little access to literature and good reading material. Every book or magazine she picked up was falling apart with mildew, or was completely out of date. Knowledge outside of herself remained a problem, and not so many of the women she knew were very interested in knowing things. Unlike them, she had made some attempt to learn the rudiments of the local language, despite the heat, which everybody complained about in the way Irish people had complex conversations about the weather.

William lay back and pondered the ceiling. Teak, teak, teak. It was everywhere. Not that he had anything against the dense, aromatic-scented wood, or indeed the many merchants who had organised men and elephants to strip the high forests and transport it down country for sale into the empire's expanding markets. The system worked perfectly, if one accepted that Burma was empire now, under Indian rule, and not merely Burma. Once the forest was stripped and flattened, the hundreds of hectares cleared of snakes, wildfowl, tigers and boars and endless greenery, once the valuable heart of it – the teak tree trunks were lumbered down country by vast teams of elephants, all was readied and improved for road and bridge-building. It was a matter of seeing the problem of the country as a whole. Of fitting pieces together so as to improve it and to improve product yields. At least, that had been his view when he and Margaret had left Ireland, a view founded on his logical admiration of groups of people who got things done, namely the British. Take rubber, those clumps of odd elastic material. There were fortunes to be made there and they could see it, and it had crossed his own mind on more than one occasion that he too might invest in some of the rubber companies springing up throughout Asia. Margaret did not encourage it, being determined to return to Ireland immediately after the three-year contract with the Eastwood Construction Company had expired. But there could be no doubt that everything the British had set their eyes on had been ingeniously exploited. They had seen the usefulness of the place – the magnificent timbers, the strange, smoky teas, the spices, the rubber, and now, recently, the prospect of oil mining. Though the pity was that they had a frightful habit of renaming things, just as they had done in Ireland, where placenames were subsumed into a new Britishness that simply did not fit with the place. He was thinking of Mandalay Palace, now called Fort Dufferin after the Viceroy of India. Somehow, the name did not sit quite right in William's mind, nor the manner in which the troops had been billeted there.

He retained strongly-happy associations with the old Palace, established during the first, confusing days after the journey from Ireland, when he and Margaret were accommodated in the Royal Pagoda Road Hotel while finishing touches were being put to their own new dwelling on Orchid Road. The suburb where they would live was new, and nestled in the foothills of the city, far enough removed that they did not hear the street sellers' voices. Only the sound of gongs from the pagodas would ever reach their home. They had wandered around the city, dazed, over-heated, and a little lonely, but much in love. Of course, their heads and hearts were easily inflamed, he admitted, and what they longed to see and hear during those first, innocent days – but did not – were exotic things like bejewelled maharajas and triumphant bugles, signs of the harmony of land and empire. It was this idea to which William had been drawn when he had signed his contract with the Eastwood Construction Company.

Margaret had been delicate at the time, her stomach easily turned by the new odours that assailed them at every turn – chillies and cloves, turmeric and durian fruit – especially as they passed by the street stalls. The only food that sustained her in her sickness was bananas, and they would buy bunches of them each day, small finger-sized clutches of greeny-skinned fruit that were sweet and ripe when unpeeled.

But as they beheld the Palace, they had both gasped involuntarily. It faced east, and all the buildings in the compound were one storey, with the number of spires over each one indicating the importance of the area below. Seeing it, they realised how far they had come from their own native culture, where there were few buildings that made anyone inhale in quick surprise. They had wandered through the walled fort, itself contained within a moat, eventually reaching the centre of the citadel to find the Palace. It had been the primary royal residence of the country's last two kings, Mindon and Thibaw. Two years later, when they had settled into life in Burma, William reflected how it seemed as if their fate was similar to that of so many other royal families, thinking of the recent deaths of the Tsar and Tsarina of Russia and their unfortunate, innocent children. Word had filtered through of revolt, a people's rebellion. The British takeover of Burma could not be compared to the like of Russia, and Thibaw and his queen had merely been exiled to India, he had heard. So really, the situation was inverted. In Russia, the people had taken back the power from a long-established autocratic though benevolent emperor, whereas in Burma the invader from another faraway land had taken power from the people, who were ruled by their own benevolent, though apparently careless, royal people.

Having got to know his man Minh rather better than his employers would approve of – so much so that Minh was also his manservant at Orchid Road – William also realised that once the British had marched into Mandalay back in the 1880s, the locals – smaller, rice and fish-fed, the least pugilistic of people – knew themselves to be no match for these rhythmically-stepping, red-uniformed giants. The country had rolled over in their wake, it seemed to William, with what the British mostly called 'insolence' being the main strand of resistance. Such insolence sometimes registered as an attitude or bearing on the part of a servant, rather than an actual action, but even it could be severely punished.

Did he realise such things when he and Margaret had set out on their great adventure? Not really, although he would have had his suspicions about layers of corruption, being Irish and having witnessed how things sometimes worked sneakily and cunningly in the Dublin administration. It was a question of survival, he concluded. On the other hand, he was not quite prepared for the level of lassitude, boredom, and indeed loneliness that afflicted so many of those from Europe who had chosen to work in the country.

Poor kings, William thought now of the Burmese royals, pulling himself up to stretch on the edge of the bed. They had surely offended nobody, only an outside powerful force which had decided that they should be got rid of. These were confusing times. Sometimes he did not wish to think too much about the problems of the world. Work was one cure, he knew, and it stopped him brooding about the justice or injustice of certain situations. But Margaret kept reading her mother's letters to him, and interesting missives they sometimes were. Her accounts of the Dublin rebellion were infinitely racier and more riveting than the anaemic, unremarkable reports that had reached them from damp, out-of-date newspapers. Nobody seemed to have a clue about what had happened or even why. He did not know quite what to think either, but it looked as if the British had delved a little too deeply into the affair, reacting with unnecessary force in Dublin. The whole thing might have blown over had it not been for the severity of their response. It was not a crime, after all, for any member of any nation to wish for autonomy and to rise up in the interests of a people's self-determination. But these men had been treated as criminals. Content as he mostly was in Burma, working with Eastwood Construction and given free rein in his collaboration on a new road north and his special project, the building of a suspension bridge, William occasionally felt trapped. And cowardly, mostly on account of some things he had witnessed when out on the job. But he would not think of them just now, not now when he remained weak.

Was he a coward? He hoped not. Any man in his right mind, with qualifications such as his, any sound fellow seeking opportunities would not have spurned the lucrative offer of professional work in a bustling, expanding outpost of the empire.

He stood up shakily and walked to the wide bedroom window, peering through the screen. A storm was brewing. The wind whittled its way through the banana leaves that clattered just beyond the balcony. The rains would fall soon, he knew, and they would be once more enclosed in a steamy, humid home as the damp sky pounded down around them, releasing insects and snakes in its wake and in the sudden silence that always followed. It was like a tap turning on suddenly, gushing violently, before eventually turning off again with the same suddenness.

It was on his first evening at the British Club that he first realised things were not as he expected them to be. Or, perhaps he had expected them to be pretty much as he found them, but had not thought through how that might make him feel. He was collected by Mark Palmer whose horse and carriage was driven by a diminutive and frail-looking man. Palmer was generally considered to be well in with the local bigwigs. Affable, it appeared to William, he was gregarious too, yet despite those qualities William could not quite warm to the man, although he couldn't pinpoint the nature of the misgiving. Something in the way Palmer laughed was slightly unsettling, and he laughed often, showing big, well-spaced teeth behind wide and fleshy lips. The skin around his eyes swelled in pouches from within which his eyes would glint as he reached the punchline of some story or other about an incident out in a remote village, usually involving one of the natives. That was it, William concluded. It was the word 'native' that bothered him, not that he was unprepared for this or unknowing. It was what the British called everybody who worked beneath them throughout the empire, and although the word was perfectly accurate it had become pejorative.

On entering the club William held his breath for a moment, overwhelmed by the heavy fug of male bodies, and an impression of quiet drunkenness. Everybody, it seemed, was keen on gin and tonic, but there was no ice, which added a paradoxical misery to the normally-delightful experience of sipping that gay drink. There they sat, his possible social companions, Major this and Brigadier that, Colonel so and so and Secretary of the such and such, whiling away the hours, pickled in the torpor of the evening. A few heads nodded in his direction.

Someone dragged himself to his feet and welcomed him, gurgling some incomprehensible welcome in an Eton baritone distorted by alcohol and cigar smoke as he slapped him on the shoulders.

A hard stone of anxiety and regret suddenly dropped in William's stomach. Was this what he had signed up for in the interests of personal advancement? Was he supposed to while away his leisure time in such company? If that was the case then he would have to ensure that he kept busy, always. And if the wives were anything like the husbands he would surely despair, for Margaret's sake.

Several old school friends from Clongowes had praised the tropics and the expatriate lifestyle. It was they who had exhorted him to travel while the going was good and a man could make money. With the war on in Europe, everything was unpredictable, they had advised late in 1914. They had influenced him, home in Ireland during the monsoon season, taking their ease, riding out, experimenting with the new automobiles that were all the rage. It was a great life, he had been assured, and once on home leave one had the wherewithal to spend freely wherever one wished throughout Europe. It would set him up for the rest of his life.

He did not linger at the club, mumbling some excuse to Palmer, who by now was well through his second glass of gin and waved him away, his face mirthful but indifferent.

'Well, you know where we are old chap, eh?'

'Yes – thanks for showing me around. Good to see the place and all that,' William replied in a desperate attempt at concealment. 'I'll walk home. It's not far,' he added.

'Anytime, anytime. And of course we're all dying to meet that little Gaelic wifey of yours, eh? Word has it she's a modern girl. Quite the enchantress, eh?'

At this, chuckles arose from within the depths of two nearby armchairs.

William pretended to cough and averted his face, which was flushing slightly. Christ, he invoked for a second time. What in hell's name had he landed them in? He thought of all Margaret's misgivings back in Ireland and of her reluctance to travel so far.

Getting to know Palmer was how he came to know Burma. The two were despatched up country some fifty miles north of Mandalay with a team of locals, comprised mostly of men from the Mon tribe, slight men with dark brown skin and tawny eyes, and several migrant Indians. They were to be in camp for six weeks, he informed Margaret, to prepare her for his absence. To his relief, Baby Henry was absorbing much of her attention in those days, but, even so, he was aware that she might face her own loneliness. She had Kyi, her woman-servant, of course, and a cook, but apart from them, was mostly dependent on herself and the company of the wives of other men who worked in the administration.

After his return from each trip, but above all from the third trip to Pyawadi, Margaret wondered at his silent withdrawal for some days afterwards. He was in really atrocious form, she noted. He would retire to his study, closing the door, closing her and anybody else out. How could he admit his awful mistake, to her who had so often warned him when they were in Dublin? He recalled her words, and those of her brother Francis, but he rarely heeded anything from Francis's lips. Francis was up to his eyes in his commitment to the idea of a new form of nationhood, and in a style that he had not approved of. William liked to be on top of every situation, to be correct in his assessments and to have his decisions received as they had been devised: with integrity. It did not sit easily for him to have to admit that he could occasionally make a mistake. To his surprise, Margaret did not burden him about his silence. If anything, she was grateful at his safe return, and happy to lie beside him in their bed each night, making no particular demands on him as she might have done in the past.

The climate was challenging, she finally admitted, before going on to regale him with some of the ways in which she had passed her weeks alone.

'I saw the fort at sunrise. It was very beautiful.'

'Why so early?'

'It is so humid during the day. I might as well rise and see something lovely rather than lie abed. Kyi accompanied me, with little Henry.'

William gave an amused grunt. 'And did Henry appreciate the great fort?'

'Oh he slept magnificently throughout! Whatever Kyi does, she has succeeded in getting him to sleep for hours on end. Don't you think he's thriving too?'

William nodded. Their baby was getting stronger by the week, and in William's six weeks' absence had become a burly infant with a pair of lungs which resonated throughout their home when he was hungry.

'We have introduced him to solids,' Margaret told him, to which William nodded vaguely. This seemed the natural order of things until she told him that the child had taken well to cook's local produce – rice, dried prawns, a little curry and even sliced green mangoes.

'Only a little,' Margaret hastened to add when she saw the expression on William's face.

'We will wish him to adjust to an Irish diet when we return. Can't you ask cook to experiment a little with a more European cuisine? Roast chicken perhaps? A little beef from time to time?'

'But the beef is poor when we can get it, and since we're here, we may as well join in the local tendencies –'

'That's exactly what we want to guard against, my darling!' William replied irritably. 'We don't want to inculcate everything – everything *native* – in our child, do we?' Immediately, he hated himself for having used that word, but he hadn't intended it badly, so much as a way of comparing the traits of one culture with another and hoping that they – being Irish and from the edge of the European continent – would be able to rear children who would fit properly back into their homeland when that time came.

'It's just food, William. It doesn't mean anything else. Don't make it more complicated than it is.'

He relented and said no more on the matter, but took pleasure in baby Henry's lusty appetite and his indiscriminate enjoyment of virtually anything he was fed. It gave rise to great correspondence between Margaret and her mother, of course, the latter being of the opinion that Margaret was correct to allow the baby to eat the food of the culture, and that as long as he thrived that was what really counted.

He remained quietly upset for days after his return from the hills, but still did not confide in Margaret. It was not that he did not wish to, but until he had settled his own feelings he could not begin to describe the event that had affected him. The place was so lush that William, who rarely paused to admire landscape, and who felt awkward describing the loveliness of things, was bewildered by it. A rough road had already been cleared, making it possible for the men to travel on horseback for miles each day within an overhang of tamarind and teak, palm, Woman's Tongue trees and umbrella trees. Most days, Palmer was tolerable enough as they moved deeper up into the hill country where there was a camp at the base of what was to be the new suspension bridge.

Nights were long-drawn processes, with the cook preparing food over a small oil-stove in the makeshift galley, and oil-lamps glimmering yellowly within the tents. There was a continuous watch for tigers. It was the one thing Palmer was forever thundering about every evening at sunset when soft blades of pink light hit the tops of the trees, the same thing to the men. If there was one slip up, he would warn, then they'd know what was good for them. The city jail might be full, but there was always room for a few more, he threatened. There was no humour in his tone when he would say this.

Planning was at an advanced stage and it was only a matter of weeks until the real work began – the digging and removing of thousands of acres of subterranean earth for the base of the bridge in preparation for the sinking by man and elephant of the enormous timber pylons. The local teams moved along, some on mules, others on horseback, yet others drawing cartloads of implements, building materials, as well as cartridges, dynamite and food. Palmer was in his element, in charge and happy to be so. He was careless in his language, William thought, especially when speaking of the men.

'You'll learn that darkies can be obstinate, Wheeler,' he once remarked, before spitting off to his right as they rode along. 'It's not in them to take orders. You have to watch them.'

William glanced to his left at his own man, Minh, riding close by, but Minh's facial expression did not alter.

'I suppose they believe it's still their country,' William responded lamely.

Palmer guffawed at this. 'That's the thing, Wheeler. They believe it's still theirs.'

When William did not reply, but instead leaned to the left as if to adjust his stirrup, Palmer rattled on.

'But it isn't theirs. It bloody isn't, and if there's one thing we're going to show these wogs – from the Lieutenant Governor right down the line – it's that we call the tune because we know what to do, dammit.'

'And they don't?'

'They absolutely don't. You said it, Wheeler.'

Palmer gave a huge pshaw of disgust, and chuckled before spitting off to his right again. William watched as the tobacco-brown gob of saliva shot straight into the foliage around them.

'If you study their history, Wheeler, you'll see they never did understand just what an immensely rich land they occupied, or, if they did, they ignored it, preferring instead to loll around in the sun, making silk and carving teak screens and what-not. For God's sake, man, they have more teak trees than any other country in the world! Then there's the religion of course – never forget the influence of religion, Wheeler – well, you couldn't, could you, being Irish ...'

He reached across to William, giving him a playful punch on the shoulder. 'Seriously though, pagodas and monasteries are all very well. Buddhism is all very well too, but it's a disincentive if a man spends his entire life thinking of merit and how to reach Nirvana, and praying he won't return in the form of a rat or a serpent. Or a woman.' He laughed at his own comedy.

At the quip William fell silent, feeling cowardly and utterly unable to command a single sentence that could in any way make the slightest dent in Palmer's views. He was impregnable, after all. He was empire, and he – William – a mere onlooker from another part of that empire, albeit an increasingly-restless part playing at being empire. He, William, was an educated Irishman with ambitions, who was ill-adjusted to the language of empire. For it was a language, he now realised, except that he did not speak it. How thick his tongue felt, how inadequate his fragile, civil sensibility in comparison to the fluent outpouring of ignorance and disparagement that flowed from Palmer's lips.

But he would try to be positive. There was the work. The work interested him, did it not? Of course it did. The work was what had lured him to travel to Burma, that and the experience it would offer him and Margaret. Though for the first time he began to think of her as poor Margaret, if she was encountering among the women what he was now learning from Palmer. He reminded himself that he must enquire of her just what the wives were like. It could make or break her contentment while in Mandalay, he now realised.

That evening they reached the campsite at Pyawadi and again Palmer gave strict instructions to the head man to set up a guarding ring of men around the site that night. They ate simply, Palmer and William and a few other engineers tucking into fried eggs and rice, followed by bananas and the vile-smelling, although delicious-tasting, Dorian fruit.

'Takes a bit of getting used to eh?' Palmer remarked, slurping back the fruit, the spaces between his large teeth filling with pulp as he gorged himself.

'I – I prefer mango myself,' William said.

'Ah, the newcomer's tropical fruit!'

The smugness of the man, William thought, wanting to mash Palmer's self-satisfied face with his right fist.

Eventually, after the lamps were lit, the camp-fire still glowing but not blazing, after the horses had been enclosed by a guarding circle of men, William relaxed a little. In his own tent, a table had been set up, and on it he spread some of the draft plans. But he could not concentrate, and inked lines and measurements were practically dancing before his eyes, beyond his comprehension, so fragmented was his mood. In the next tent he could hear Palmer rattling on to one of his companions, his account of his story punctuated at intervals by great yelps and guffaws. He was speaking about an English civil servant down in Rangoon who had broken rank and married a Burmese girl. Not that he was the only one, he remarked, but even so it didn't do. They were the most comical-looking pair, William overheard, she was outfitted in the style of a lady from the Home Counties, replete with large-brimmed hat, and all the accoutrements of dress that one would expect, with such dainty lace gloves covering her little brown paws. Except for the fact that they looked ridiculous on her, for God's sake, she had this simian little face too, a little brown thing who looked to be straight from the trees, it was so ridiculous, so damn ridiculous, the fellow must have been off his head on too much warm gin, he rambled on before eventually, gradually, falling silent.

William shifted and twisted for an hour more before he slept. The camp bed was uncomfortable. He listened to the night, which was, as ever, active and noisy. He was aware of creatures moving around them, of how isolated their group of men was in the forest, of how there could very well be a tiger or two sizing up an opportunity. *Tyger, Tyger, burning bright* ... he whispered softly, remembering the poem he had studied when Fr Hubbard had taught him English at Clongowes. Except that the poem was about creation and not really about a tiger, he seemed to recall. Well, here he was now with the evidence of cosmic creation all around him, burning brightly in the night, the bewitching, uneasy hiss and shift of earth and foliage, as this and that creature slithered and prowled, hunted and preyed all the long night on the mysterious lonely planet on which he found himself in his life.

He awoke the following morning to a livid shriek of pain. God in heaven, he thought, ripping himself off the camp bed and tearing back the tent flap. His eyes fell first on Palmer, who was prancing like a lunatic over a Burmese man who cowered near the galley, clinging to an empty pan. Palmer wrenched the pan from the man's hand.

'You idiot!' he roared, striking him with the pan. 'You scalded my left hand with boiling water! Can't you people follow the simplest instruction or see two inches ahead without stumbling or tripping? Couldn't you see me right there? I asked for hot – HOT – not boiling water, you stupid ape! All I wanted was to wash my hands before I touched the miserable breakfast you've prepared. Is that too much? Is it? Is it?'

The man was trembling. He scrambled on the ground like a small animal about to be beaten but used to it, attempting to get to his feet, at the same time shielding his face from the onslaught.

'No master, no master, it is not too much,' the miserable man replied.

'You know something? I think you should receive fifteen lashes for this, but not now, boy, not until we return to base. I won't forget, and in the meantime –' He continued to strike the man repeatedly with the pan on the shoulders, along his back, on his thin hips. The entire campsite had gone quiet and the men looked on, expressions varying depending on their station, from indifference or astonishment, to outright fear.

'I sorry master! Sor-ree master! I thought water was for *lahpet*. Forgive.'

But Palmer had lost the run of himself. He did not stop striking the man.

'I did not ask for *lahpet*, you jabbering moron! I do not drink *lahpet* until I have washed my hands of every vile germ I may have picked up from contact with you lot.'

Palmer's normally ruddy-cheeked face had turned white with temper, William noticed, as the onslaught began again. He struck once more, now aiming for the man's head, the sound of the pan against the servant's skull like the sounds that emanated from some of the monasteries, or on the streets when the boy monks were out at dawn looking for alms.

'How do you like that boy, eh? The sound of tin on bone, yes, that's it – pure bone, the head of a total numbskull!'

But William could no longer bear it, and suddenly sprang forward, grasping Palmer's wrist, wrenching it back and twisting hard until he relinquished the pan. At first, Palmer did not realise who had halted him, and he resisted, readying himself to attack another opponent.

'No!' William shouted, tightening his grip and quickly catching Palmer's other arm to twist it up behind his back. He was bigger and stronger than the Englishman, and quickly quietened him.

'*Wheeler!*' Palmer was furious. 'You'll regret this interference – it's none of your damn business!'

'You could have killed him. You weren't going to stop.'

Breathless from exertion, Palmer shook off William and glared for some moments at the servant. The man, blood running from the side of his head, dragged himself away on his knees, before collapsing with a low groan. Nobody moved to attend him. The workers stood as if frozen, though already sweat had broken out on their faces and bare arms, their eyes moving between the injured man and Wheeler's face.

'One life more or less makes no difference out here, Wheeler. You'll soon learn that.'

'That man needs a doctor, Palmer – look at him!'

Palmer studied him a moment. He rummaged in one of his shorts pockets and brought out a packet of cigarettes. Slowly, he withdrew one, struck a match, lit it and inhaled.

'The thing is, Wheeler – William, old boy – these blighters are as tough as old nails. A doctor for that moron? Don't make me fucking laugh.'

William went for him then. He could not restrain his temper nor hold back from the essential pleasure of really throttling Palmer. He had him on the ground, with the dust and ash from the previous day's fire rising around them in clouds, and his two hands had Palmer about the throat. He was squeezing hard, so hard he could feel the man's Adam's Apple beneath the bristly casing of unshaven neck-skin, and he watched, as if he had risen above his own body, as Palmer attempted to knee him in the groin but failed; he watched as the face beneath his was turning purple, the eyeballs gradually bulging even as the skin of the eyelids tightened. He felt also the sweetness of a revenge he had not known he needed to extract, against Palmer, against Burma, against India, and against an entire nation which had undermined every country it had ever entered, leaving each enfeebled, causing wars and in the case of his own land – famine – creating a chain metal weight of systematic dispossession around the globe. How could he ever have forgotten so much?

As he held onto Palmer, his thoughts sank as deeply as his emotions, until suddenly he felt someone grip the back of his shirt, and someone else grabbing his shoulder, and before he knew it he was dragged away from his victim, who lay gasping, supine.

It almost did not end well for William. The trek back to Mandalay was not for another ten days, and in that interval he and Palmer worked in a state of mostly rigid silence. The man Palmer had attacked with the pan had recovered quickly enough, but that was not the point. William tried to apologise to Palmer, but in vain. He hardly expected the man to respond to the gesture anyway. A physical attack on a compatriot, as Palmer insisted on calling himself, to distinguish between the Burmese and their overlords, was intolerable. The example it gave, for one thing, apart from the near permanent injury William had done to his throat – Palmer could only whisper for a week after the attack – as well as the personal humiliation and the sheer effrontery of it. What the hell was he thinking of? Palmer wanted to know.

'If you think you're going to get yourself in favour with these wogs by standing up for one of 'em, you've got another think coming, Wheeler. The Burmese don't care much for loyalty – they won't be loyal to you, me or anyone else. It's all about what they can get out of the situation, see? They wheedle and cower and smile and grovel, then they pretend to work, and behind it all they resent us, despite all the benefits we've brought to this stinking hellhole. Get that into your thick Irish head and you might do well enough for yourself out here. Otherwise, go back to your own godforsaken bog in BallyMacCeltic.'

But on the day he arrived back from camp William was so weary he had not even the energy to tell Margaret just then what had happened. It was a question of getting Kyi to draw a bath for him and of asking Margaret to tell cook to prepare something reasonably fresh-tasting for dinner. Fried chicken. Rice. A sweet pineapple afterwards. He could not think. He could not think ahead either. Everything could wait until he had slept and until the next day.

There was the inevitable meeting with the Eastwood Construction people, a full board of men settled comfortably into wicker chairs, gin and tonics to hand, as William was interviewed regarding what had transpired upcountry. Palmer had already filed a full report, prepared while in camp and then transported by one of the men on horseback directly back to the city. William had heard him dictate it to the coolie entrusted with letter-writing – decrying his behaviour, his lack of fellowship and his failure to understand how the system worked in everybody's best interest. Palmer sat among his inquisitors and watched William as he attempted to defend himself, as he questioned the flagrant beating of native men for minor, accidental misdemeanours.

'They are not even misdemeanours,' he pleaded. 'We are speaking of the purely accidental.'

He expected to have his contract severed, and wondered if Margaret would be annoyed or relieved. He expected that she would be mildly relieved, in the end, at not having to fulfil the three years in Burma. She would certainly be astonished when he told her the story.

It mystified him that his contract was not dissolved. There was no sanction at all, beyond the mildest of repudiations in a memo delivered to the house. What it concluded was that circumstances in camp can sometimes be difficult and that the Europeans working for the Eastwood Construction Company must pull solidly together. It was in everybody's best interest, the note concluded, and they hoped that a man of his intelligence would understand that.

They endured. He told Margaret, and she listened, horrified. They endured as most of the other couples endured Burma, fulfilling their contract, making the best of things, occasionally feeling themselves to be adventurous and full of courage, when in fact their presence there had nothing to do with courage. When the time came to depart from Mandalay, Margaret wept openly as she said goodbye to Kyi. The little maid's eyes also watered, though there was not the same outpouring as rolled down Margaret's cheeks. Their baggage had already been sent ahead to the train, and all that remained was to close up the house with Kyi and cook, to hand back keys and to take their leave.

In spite of every difficulty – of climate, sickness, adjustment, custom – they left with a pang in their hearts which felt like a deeply-lodged thorn. It was a little like having fallen in love, Margaret thought, so that the peculiar, uncomfortable things about the person were now oddly desirable now that you were leaving one another.

Even William, whose difficulties with Palmer had affected too much of his work, knew that they were turning away from something: a people, a climate that twisted and churned within every cell of their bodies, then an assault on the senses that rendered anything they had ever before encountered somewhat anodyne. But they left.

The train to Rangoon was packed, and even in First Class things remained uncomfortable and clammy. Henry and his sister Flora – now entrusted for the journey to the exclusive care of both parents – twisted and turned restlessly, so that Margaret found it difficult to hold her patience. Four days on, they set sail at last, pulled out from the port and into the Yangon River. She watched for an hour or more as the city retreated, remembering how she had watched Kingstown in retreat on the autumn afternoon three years before. Here though, unlike the brilliant blackness of the Irish Sea which had seemed to her then fanciful eyes like black silk flashed with moonlight, the waters of the Yangon as they approached open sea were milky and unclear as if fathoms of sand and sludge were constantly stirred up and moiling in and out with the tides of the Andaman Sea.

3

Dublin

William had made up his mind. He was going to buy an automobile. No sooner had the family arrived in Dublin after the passage from Burma than he was like a man possessed. It was as if all that had happened over the past three years had been a dream and he was now determined to attach himself as quickly as possible to the modern reality of his homeland in 1918. And what a bewildering new place it was, he thought, feeling great satisfaction at being free of the place he had almost loved, but had fallen short of so doing, because of that damn Palmer. After the incident at the camp, Palmer had made William's working life as difficult as possible, even attempting to isolate him at the Eastwood Company clubhouse from the social companionship it offered.

Henry, now three, was able to grasp the significance of this decision, having been perched in his father's arms and frequently shown the wonders of motorcars on St Stephen's Green where people still clustered to watch the latest fashionable model wheezing and drumming past the Royal College of Surgeons, towards Grafton Street. The little boy would point excitedly, doing what his father actually wanted to, but could not by virtue of his age and station. These motorcars were usually controlled by an important-looking gent, shoulders squared, both hands firmly gripping the high steering wheel as he carefully eased his way past horses and jaunting cars, bicycles and gawkers.

Margaret, while pleased at William's proposal, was preoccupied with restoring the house at Herbert Place to a state in which it felt homely again. During their absence, her mother had overseen the lease of the property to two elderly gentlemen who ran the Concert Rooms on Brunswick Street. Although perfectly mannerly, indeed delightful company according to Mrs Ward, they had not bothered about the upkeep of any aspect of the house except the piano, and by the time the Wheelers returned and the gentlemen had vacated the property, there was a great deal for Margaret to attend to. The piano was gleaming, if out of tune, but the occasional furnishings in that room showed distinct signs of having supported a great deal of entertainment, between water rings on the tables, to cigar burns on the arms of the chairs, as well as other, unidentifiable stains on the carpet and rugs. So, she was content to have William pursue whatever escapade he wished. It gave her time to brighten their home but also to adjust to her home city.

One of her first decisions was to place the brass gong, which had been transported to Burma and back, in a position of some importance in the long, arched hallway. She positioned it on the teak table which was among the furniture that had also accompanied them, most of it arriving a week later into Dublin Port. Other items that she had favoured were placed with a new, almost talismanic, significance throughout the house: a peacock-patterned ginger jar, a set of antique jade figurines depicting different aspects of a struggle between two men and a tiger, and a lacquered drinks cabinet.

Despite months and months of homesickness after they reached their house in Mandalay, despite the huge sense of strangeness and the uncomfortable feeling that she would never again feel quite herself, she found it equally unsettling to be back in Dublin. There was so much to remember, and some things to forget, not the least of them that dreadful Palmer creature with his hideous teeth and ever-flapping lips, and the ill-feeling towards William which had lingered like a poison through the remainder of his contract. She wanted to balance these, to carefully sift the past three years' experiences as she worked and cleaned. Because work and clean she had to, furiously.

Every fibre of her being itched for physical work of some kind, and the often sedentary life she had led in Mandalay had taken its toll on her body and spirit. She wanted to be strong and vital again, to do things – not only to be a good mother to her children – but to change something, although she was not sure what.

Back in Dublin, Margaret had immediately employed a housemaid, although not a cook. The maid was called Peggy, and came from Monaghan and was prepared to do some cooking. She had had a fine class of country house to work in before this one, she assured Margaret, but it was a house of men, with no wife, and her work increased to such an extent that eventually she felt she might seek her working fortunes elsewhere. With an excellent and clearly reluctantly-written reference to hand, she had presented herself one afternoon to Margaret, who quickly realised that this was a maid she would be able to tolerate. Moreover, she seemed to take to Flora, who was by then a sturdy fourteen-month-old. She advised Margaret promptly that it might be wiser if she ignored her mother's remonstrations regarding Flora's clumsy speech to date. If anything the little girl was often silent and liked to point to indicate her wishes.

'Sure one of the childer in Monaghan didn't open his beak until he was two!'

'Really?'

'Some of them are happy to say nothing with all the chat that's around them. Or a wee bit lazy. Nothing more.'

Flora was a sweet child. Even during the thunderstorms, during raging monsoon and violent floods, when the household on Orchid Road was battened and shuttered and sometimes even the natives were ill-at-ease, Flora slept through it all. Unlike Henry, who from the outset had been alert to everything and rarely slept, thus ensuring that Margaret and William developed grey circles beneath their eyes after his first few months.

Her mind kept retreating to Burma. During the monsoon it had sometimes felt as if they were once again trapped on the outward-bound ship as it had tracked its way through a violent storm down the French coast. At such times she felt the alien presence of this culture bearing down on them, pushing them away as much as it appeared to need William's talents.

And since William's malaria, in certain ways Margaret felt he had never quite been restored to his old form, that his moods were sometimes a little testy, that he sickened more easily than hitherto and had generally lost enthusiasm even for his important work. Of course, she reasoned, Palmer was partly to blame for that. But she bore up, resolving that once she had organised the household and got everything in running order, with she and Peggy establishing a sound arrangement between them, that she would finally turn her attention to the most neglected aspect of her life: her education. One should never look back for long – one should always try to see a new way forward – and with that in mind she would have to speak to William.

On the day William decided to visit the Ballsbridge Automobile Centre she kissed him on the cheek and waved him off. With Peggy's help she had decided to strip the surface of the main reception room floor, where it was visible outside the centre carpet. The old, heavily-stained carpet having been removed and the new one she had ordered from Arnotts not having arrived, it seemed a golden opportunity to remake the room, from the heavy oak plank floor up to the coved and moulded ceiling. William had advised her to get a craftsman to do the job, and in any case this was not suitable work for her. But she insisted.

'William, I want something to *do!*'

'But darling, you have our children. Don't they keep you busy?'

'Yes but –'

'But nothing. You mustn't tire yourself out with such physical labours, Margaret. This is not the kind of work a wife should undertake.'

But he knew from experience not to press the matter further. Margaret had sealed her lips in the trenchant way that signalled when her mind was set. Just as he had resolved to go out and buy the very latest 10hp Peugeot with hand-painted wooden frames, four-wheel brakes and a beautiful klaxon horn, so too was she determined to strip the floor.

Peggy, whose brother was a carpenter, knew something about what the work entailed. Two kinds of sandpaper were required, one coarse and the other of a lighter quality. These were purchased in Capel Street later that morning, along with turpentine and linseed oil. All these Peggy bore into the house around lunchtime.

'Here, Mrs,' she said, laying her goods on the kitchen table. 'You can decide on the colour of the stain another day. That'll be the least of our worries I'd say.'

At this point both children were bawling and querulous at Margaret's heels, hungry for lunch, their hunger compounded by the fact that she had not been lavishing them with the usual attention, so preoccupied was she with the reception room. They had trailed after her all morning, little Flora falling back on her bottom each time she tried to keep up with Henry, who teased her by drawing her along after him a little more, before letting go of her hand so that she again plonked back on her bottom.

They quietened down after Peggy had stuffed a good rabbit stew into their mouths. She believed in filling children up as one might a horse's nosebag with grain – put plenty in and the creatures gave no trouble for hours. The stew she had prepared the evening before, anticipating another day of slight unpredictability in the

Wheeler household when she never knew for certain where her attentions might be directed.

The family had not completely unpacked their trunks, yet already young Mrs Wheeler was for reforming the entire house before getting her foreign clothes sorted, washed, hung out or given away. But at least in this household there was less laundry, Peggy noted – much of it women's things, which were easier handled and lighter. It was very different from her previous employer's house in Monaghan, where the men came and went like kings, in and out of that smoky kitchen, and the only thing that ever silenced them was the young son not returning from the war. Oh that quietened them, his death, and the mistake of his ever having gone over beyond in the first place. That would quieten a body for ever, she mused, thinking of Arthur's father and then of Arthur's poor young fiancé. With the boy's death she could not tolerate the grief in that household any longer because it was as if all the light had been snuffed out.

She could see herself getting on well with this new mistress, younger than she by five years or so, and not a bit like many women of her standing. She seemed more restless, Peggy observed, as if there was something eating at her which had not yet been satisfied.

In the early afternoon, both children were put down for a sleep, and Margaret and Peggy set to work, the former in the new trouser skirts which, she said, gave her far more freedom of movement. This article of clothing, Margaret – in a burst of enthusiasm to acquire the latest fashions – had rushed to buy within a week of their return.

Peggy looked doubtful. 'I doubt thon trouser skirts will catch on.'

'Why ever not?' Margaret demanded, 'It's a useful garment. I couldn't possibly be down on my knees doing work like this in a skirt.'

They set to labour, Peggy at one corner of the rectangular room and Margaret at the other, armed with a supply of toughest workman's sandpaper. Neither had ever had to sand a floor, so Peggy suggested respectfully that it might be an idea if they were to draw the rough paper down in straight lines, rather than attacking the old varnish in a circling motion. They ought to go with the grain of the wood, she advised, as Margaret worked like a demon at first, pouring her strength into the task.

'I think we don't need to go so hard, Mrs,' Peggy cautioned.

'But it's a hard wood.'

'The varnish on it isn't, though. Gently does it Mrs, gently. We just show that stuff who's boss and it will lift easy enough.'

Two hours passed before they reached the bottom of the room. They had kept up with one another's rhythm throughout, gradually building up a slow, deliberate, but light stroke as they brushed the sandpaper up and down, up and down, until the paler wood tone beneath years of accreted varnish revealed itself. Margaret did not once stop. Her underclothes were stuck to her back, and rivulets of sweat ran from her hairline and down the front of her neck.

'It's beautiful!' she gasped, wiping her forehead with her arm. 'It reminds me of Burma. The smell of real wood. Hard wood. And do you know something, Peggy? If I get any warmer, I'll have an attack of prickly heat again!'

'It will look like something when we get the stain on,' said Peggy, with a cough. Fine dust and varnish sediments floated in shafts of sunlight as she set to work again.

Margaret sniffed the woody odour and the tang of old varnish. Burma. To her astonishment, sometimes she even missed that country.

The women stopped to refresh themselves. In the kitchen, Peggy pushed the kettle onto the hotplate. A quick drizzle of water jumped from the spout and spattered and danced in hot bubbles on the top of the range. The kettle stirred to life. Margaret flopped down on the old couch to one side of the hearth while Peggy busied herself with cups and saucers. They had made progress. Now all that remained were the two shorter sides of the room, but they would have to leave that until the next day. The kettle was singing, then that sound deepened to a well-heated growl before the water eventually began to buck and leap within the heavy vessel. Peggy wet the teapot, added tea, then poured a steaming torrent from the kettle. The sound of feet from an upstairs bedroom reminded them that Henry and, most likely, Flora, had awoken from their naps. But Peggy would see to them, Margaret thought, sipping her tea, and starting to feel drowsy by the warm range. The two women fell silent. It had been a vigorous afternoon. This, she thought, was so different to her relationship with Kyi, who would have practically swooned in shock had Margaret attempted to sit companionably in a room with her.

A short while later Margaret glanced quickly into the reception room before closing the doors behind her. She walked a little wearily along the hallway towards the stairs. Her back ached. What wouldn't she give for the kind of extravagant bath Kyi used to provide whenever she was feeling particularly tired. But there was no chance of that here, she thought, remembering how Kyi used to run a deep tub of warm water and invite her to step out of her bath towel and immerse herself in its comforting depths. Kyi spoke little English beyond the language of service, and reverted to her own tongue as she bathed Margaret. Sometimes Margaret suspected that the small, stocky maid from the high hills recognised how fraught she was feeling, especially when William's life was in such danger and there seemed nothing to be done but wait it out, to see if the fever and delirium might eventually pass without killing him. On the evening when the fever finally dropped and his pulse slowed to a normal rate, he had been enormously weakened. Even so, Margaret felt sweet relief. He would live, she thought. He would live and she would not be left alone with one child and another in the womb, in the dark and bristling heart of the Orient. She would be a better wife to him; she would put more of her heart into their life together. But Kyi led her softly to the bathroom and pointed to the bath. Her brown eyes were telling her to bathe. Once in the water, chin on knees, arms wrapped around her shins, she luxuriated in the abandonment of all thought as the maid soaped and rinsed her back over and over again. The child in her belly turned slowly as she sat there, and that feeling also comforted her. She was never worried about the unborn little one. Some instinct made her believe that this child knew exactly what it was doing from the moment it had been conceived, unlike her first pregnancy which had been difficult throughout and had included one small emergency after particularly passionate intimacy with William. But she did not miscarry, and after a few days' bed rest all was well and William did not dare approach her for the rest of her term. After the bath the woman held up a heavy cotton towel and wound it carefully, lightly, around Margaret's body, so much so that the intimate attention made her suddenly weep. Before she knew it, tears were hopping down her face and short, sharp breaths sputtered from her.

'Oh – God!' she had gulped.

Kyi looked her in the eyes, her own black-fringed eyelashes suddenly widening at the outburst, and said something in her own language. She kept repeating this, her firm hand on Margaret's shoulders, the other one then moving to her belly and holding it there until she grew quiet again, dried her eyes on the towel and slid into the black silk pyjamas with their pattern of Green Peafowl or *Daung* which William had bought for her birthday that year. He was such a good and thoughtful husband, she thought, to go to the trouble of ordering them from the best silk-weaver in Mandalay.

Since the return to Ireland, they were all she wanted to wear at night, because as long as she could wear them, she could feel attached to something that had, even in its difficulties, been incredibly important. Perhaps also, she suspected, it had something to do with both her children having grown inside her in that country, and come into life beneath its hot, stinging skies. Burma had changed her life, even if she had done little else but keep house in an indolent style and be a mother. But those activities were not the point. It was the place, and the system which fully despised the culture, which had affected her. How could it be otherwise, she thought. Out there she grew up and learned some things. Before, in Ireland, despite her mother's activities and political commitments, there had not been enough time for learning. This was her true hunger. While in Burma she attempted to absorb the rudiments of the language – without much success – yet by so doing made herself slightly less welcome in the expatriate circles. Language basics were superfluous and few of the ladies of her acquaintance saw any point in learning Burmese. In the Reading Circle, for example, which convened once a month in someone's home to discuss one of the latest batch of uplifting novels somebody had selected and shipped out, the conversation often centred on the trouble with local maids, their inability to get things just right in a domestic setting. *Of course, they're not used to it,* someone might say with a sigh, or *What can we expect? The Mon are tribespeople at heart, better off bringing one of our own girls out, if only they could be persuaded to travel!* So Margaret learned not to discuss her interest in the language, just as at home in Ireland there had been certain social cabals in which it was most unfashionable to declare a concern for their own language, Irish. How far apart their countries were, she had often mused, and yet how close in this one respect at least.

That evening at dinner, William was momentarily distracted by Margaret's excitement about the sanding of the reception room floor, and cast a critical eye over the result of the day's labours.

'I say, you've surprised me darling. Yet again.'

'You always did underestimate me, William,' Margaret replied softly.

'It's just that – you know my feelings about ladies doing such work – I'd be ashamed to have our friends know that this is how you spend your time.'

Margaret said nothing, but steered him towards the dining room to eat.

'What about the automobile?' she enquired casually.

'There's a fair choice.'

He sat down, opened his napkin and waited for Peggy's arrival with a laden silver tray.

He wanted to get a vehicle that was just right for them, he told Margaret, so that they would be able to motor in comfort and style. They would be able to take Sunday afternoon trips out of the city, to Wicklow and Kildare. Margaret, exhausted from the day's work, listened and nodded. It would be wonderful, she agreed with some excitement, to drive out with no horse, to transform the coach house into a new garage – apparently the French called it a 'gar-aahj', softly emphasising the second syllable – and how marvellous to dispense with the tram and the omnibus and simply control one's own destiny. How modern it seemed. They laughed with pleasure at the thought of modernity taking place in their lives. Surely, they lived on the very foremost perimeter of progress, gliding into the future every minute of every day of every year.

They were centuries ahead of life in other parts of the world, she concluded, and human science and advancement could only be to the general good of humanity.

There was a slight pause in the conversation and William helped himself to a bowl of buttered mashed carrots and parsnips.

'William,' she said suddenly, leaning forward and fiddling with her fork.

'Yes dear?'

'I've been thinking.'

'Nothing strange about that – doesn't do any harm at all, according to the best doctors!'

'Seriously, William, I've been thinking about something important.'

He put down his own knife and fork and looked at her expectantly.

'I want to go to university, William.'

She spoke the words quickly. There. It was out in the open.

He looked at her blankly before the words formed in his mouth.

'You *what*?'

'University. It's high time I had an education.'

William pushed his dinner plate away as if he had suddenly lost his appetite. The meal – Peggy's roast chicken and savoury stuffing – lay unfinished.

'What the hell –'

'I've always wanted to learn more – you know that, William. There's still time for me to –'

'To what? To make a fool of yourself at University College? It's all *men*, you know, male students.'

'Not exclusively, dear.'

She was trying to hold her patience, to be calm and strategic about the matter. She could get a place, she knew that for certain. She was qualified to attend University College Dublin, to take lectures in French and English or even in Irish. There was no rule that stated only very young women need apply. Moreover, they could afford it. So, as far as she was concerned, everything was already in place for her personal advancement, except for the matter of persuading William. He leaned forward and peered into her face with real curiosity, as if studying a hitherto undiscovered species.

'Are you unhappy, Margaret? Is there something that makes you so discontented you wish to leave the home every day to attend classes? Am I – are we, for I think of the children too – not *enough* for you?'

Frankly, yes, she wanted to reply enthusiastically, but then thought the better of it. Of course William and the children were enough. It was not so simple. On the scales of justice it should not be a contest between one aspect of a woman's life and another. Even Mother had said that. In fact, she was always saying it, and when she had returned from her latest London trip to the Suffragettes, she had told Margaret that all women who were able, were honour-bound to change things, to make sacrifices to do so. After all, women had recently been granted the right to vote. That was progress, but it had come with qualifications, since the women had to be thirty years or more and the legislators wanted to be certain that their brains were mature enough to take the momentous decision of voting correctly.

'Of course you are enough. That was never in question. But – you know how you were able to attend university to study as an engineer? You do remember that, don't you? How wonderful it was? And all that you learned there?'

She was being very patient, and she believed her patience would yield the desired response. 'So it is for me. I need something else.'

'You need something else?' He spoke the last word as if it was part of a new language he had never before encountered.

'Yes dear. Something else.'

'But what about your children?'

Something broke in her then and her face turned pink with frustration. Suddenly they were *her* children.

'Why are you doing this, William?'

He was the picture of innocent bafflement, but she pressed on.

'Why are you using the children as pawns in some – some hideous game?'

'This is not a game and I have never been more serious,' he said quietly.

Then the real row got underway. In the kitchen, Peggy could hear raised voices as she prepared the children for bed. To protect them she began to sing a complicated air she was fond of, the words to which she only half-knew.

Where Lagan stream sings lullaby
There blows a lily fair …

Oh it was a romantic air all right, Peggy considered as she hummed and sang, though there was little romance in Herbert Place that particular evening. The pair of them were strong, but so different, she had noted, which could only mean one thing: trouble.

She pulled off Henry's liberty bodice and replaced it with his night vest, over which she drew his flannelette pyjama tops. Little Flora was cooing contentedly into one of the kitchen saucepans, occasionally banging it with a large wooden spoon as Peggy sang.

And like a love-sick leannán-shee
She has my life in thrall.
Nor life I owe nor liberty
For Love is Lord of all.

Love was definitely not Lord of all, Peggy decided, as a livid shriek of rage ripped through the house and penetrated the kitchen. Henry turned his head and pointed to the doorway.

'Mother and Father are playing,' Peggy announced, then resumed her song.

In the diningroom, William mounted protest after protest against his wife's latest notion. He wondered aloud what had happened while they were in Burma to make her return in such an unpredictable state of mind. Was this discontent and rebellion formenting when he and the men were up to their eyes in tropical foliage, unreliable coolies, leeches, snakes and the constant danger of other deadly creatures as they assessed the territories for the new bridge at Pyawadi? He wished now he had never left her alone for weeks on end, he said bitterly. She was obviously not suited to isolation in a foreign country.

At this she held her hand up and stopped him.

'Of course I was not suited to isolation in a foreign country. No normal person thrives in such a mad and – and *stupid* place.'

'But you had the company of ladies whenever you wished to have it.'

'Indeed I had. And you? You know what most of them were like.'

She had had her fill of ladies' trips to this pagoda and that pagoda, to the endless pleasantries which she imagined were acts of concealment for some of them. She was sick of pious talks and by God she was sick of the sight of the golden lions perched as tradition would have it outside the pagodas and temples. She had looked, exclaimed and remembered diligently the beauty of such places – for they were vivid and profoundly contemplative if one was left alone to enjoy them – but she felt that she might as well have been an orchid in a hothouse each time she returned to their own spacious but verandah-darkened home. She would mount the steps to be greeted by the groundsman who would warn her, with a tragic face, about the python in the garden and how she must not walk past a certain point in the grounds. It was true. There was a small python somewhere in the garden. It took weeks to finally expose the serpent. She regretted that the men had killed it, having observed them from an upstairs window, through the screen, as three of them surrounded it and quickly used their shotguns. The largely harmless creature writhed horribly, it was ghastly to observe the massive strength of the head and the powerful undulations of the greeny-yellow body as it gradually slipped into death. Afterwards, one of the natives came with a machete and decapitated it, carrying the trophy head home to his village, where it was no doubt stewed in a pot and an aphrodisiac potion concocted for the men.

Margaret had poured herself a half-tumbler of neat gin, lit a cigarette and wondered about the richness that was all around her, which – she knew – she was approaching, by virtue of her station and circumstances, from completely the wrong route. Pythons, banana trees, teak wood, incense, the gentle child-rearing practices, but also the people's labour – all these impinged on her consciousness and the result was that she felt more removed than she would like to have been. If she had to be in Burma she wanted something more. Just like now, in Ireland, she was again seeking that extra layer of what was indefinable.

'I don't know what more I can do for you, Margaret,' William eventually said. His expression was unforgiving, as if she had grossly offended him.

'I would simply like to have your understanding.'

'It's difficult to understand.'

'At least try.'

'And if I refuse to go along with this absurd plan?'

'You know well what the answer to that is, my dear.'

Without William's blessing, without his money to pay the fees, she might as well forget the idea. She would retreat like a flower folding its petals in the evening, and live obscurely and quietly while the great world and their newly-unsettled country expanded all around her. Surely he knew that? She felt weak and resentful at the lack of force she possessed. Few decisions were hers alone to make, it seemed, beyond the realm of the children.

But William did not understand the situation. He frowned and suddenly looked very despondent.

'So – you would just – go ahead?'

'Of course not, William! How could I?'

It seemed he had not heard her. Or had not grasped the truth of a woman's life.

'You are thinking of returning to your mother then? You have no need of me and are prepared to return to your first home and desert me? Margaret!'

His face had blanched and he clenched his fists, banging them together in anguish as he puzzled the matter. It was a disaster, he thought. She would do this – she would leave him for the sake of an *education*?

Now she was reaching the nub of the matter. She regarded him and pitied him. It astonished her to think that he was so vulnerable, despite all the bluster and argument, as to assume she would up sticks and return to her mother.

'That's a ludicrous idea, William. It has never – not once – crossed my mind. Why on earth would I return to Mother and Francis? They would drive me mad in their different ways! Or don't you understand?'

'What don't I understand?'

'That if you oppose my further education then that will be an end to it. I would not accept the situation happily, that goes without saying, but William – my dearest!'

The sight of him distressed her. She knew she was soft-hearted, sometimes to her own disadvantage. *The terror was that she might leave.* To think a woman had so much power and not know it. To think she had achieved this power by a circuitous and almost secretive route. Oh, if the world could only change and men and women be progressive enough in their relations to allow one another whatever freedoms they desired! But that would never be. Men now and men in the far future of their country would still be in thrall to women's bodies; they would always need to return to their own souls as if through an ancient labyrinth, and that labyrinth was woman. It was neither a fault nor a strength, Margaret concluded. It was an aspect of a natural strategy that had taken millennia to evolve and her all this time to recognise.

William watched in silence as she pondered. In the distance Peggy was still singing. The haunting melody drifted from the kitchen, along the hallway, a spectral sound that – although they could not hear the words – carried bewitching hints of love gained and perhaps lost.

'You – would not leave?' William asked.

The first stirrings of peace pushed through their differences.

'Never.'

'In that case –'

But she stopped him. 'Say nothing now, William. You felt vehemently opposed to the question only a while ago, so now you should think about it overnight. Perhaps before you leave to buy the motorcar tomorrow morning you could tell me your decision. That is all I ask.'

She was exhausted. After the children had gone to bed and William was reading in his study, she padded quietly to the kitchen. Peggy sat by the range, turning the heel on a sock. Her four needles clicked and clacked in the soft-lit room and the open range threw light and shadows at the ceiling. Above her head a line of laundry stiffened in the heat. Margaret threw herself into a chair beside Peggy.

'You must be tired Mrs,' Peggy remarked, glancing at her.

Margaret nodded.

'I am so tired, I want to die.'

'Ah now, that's foolish talk. You're not Madame Bernhardt on the stage yet!'

'But it's true,' Margaret replied peevishly.

For a moment, the other woman said nothing, but knitted on, clicketty-clicketty-clicketty, the rhythm of it rolling lightly between them.

'Nobody ever said marriage was aisy.'

At this Margaret burst into tears. It wasn't that she didn't love him, she confided, because she did. But he could be quite resistant to change when it concerned others, although not himself. At this, Peggy smiled. Men wanted things all their own way and it was only after a lot of arguing or cajoling that women got anywhere. Margaret went on, stopping every so often to blow her nose. The problem was no intelligent woman could consign herself to a life of conversations in which cajoling was the female method for getting things done. She wasn't even *good* at cajoling, she added, not like some women were.

'You need to go to bed Mrs,' Peggy finally said, putting down her knitting.

'You're right. I'm exhausted after the work on that floor, but to listen to William later – it was all too much!'

'Of course it was.'

'Peggy?'

'Yes?'

'Can I ask a favour? A big one?'

'You can ask anything you want, Mrs, but as you know asking doesn't always mean getting.'

'Would you – would you mind – washing my back if I were to take a bath?'

At this Peggy stirred, as if nonplussed.

'I've never been asked to do *that* before, but I don't see why not,' she said cautiously. 'If you don't mind me doing it.'

'Why else would I ask you?'

As the bath was running and Margaret undressed, she thought she heard the gong being struck softly in the hallway. She strained her ears. Yes, that was it, the humming, tinny, high tone, audible and resonating through the house, even over the sound of pouring water. Then she spotted William through the open doorway as he ascended the stairs. The moon was gibbous and cast a translucent fan on the stairway. He passed through it, like a man from another world. He too was tired, she suspected. Adapting to Ireland had not come easily to either of them. There were changes afoot, not alone in the manner of his work, but in people's attitudes. He noticed it in the office, where even the secretaries spoke about independence, and 'democracy', a word which everybody in Burma had loathed whenever it reached their eyes or ears, usually through newspapers such as *The Mandalay Star*. Now too, in Ireland, the families who had lost sons in the Great War were seen as different from those who mourned for the Volunteers in the Rising. It was as if people did not know what to do with soldiers who returned, often limbless, blind or with parts of their skulls replaced with sheets of curved metal.

She was sorry to have missed the Rising and so was William. How unlucky to have been out in the heart of the colonies just at the moment when the nation of Ireland, England's nearest colony, was attempting to be born in the maddest of ways. And now, that born thing was alive and squalling and it was so hard to know what to think about it or what to do with it. Oh, there was so much to know, so much yet to discover, she concluded, slipping into a robe as she entered the bathroom.

Steam billowed out onto the landing as William stuck his head around the door.

'Bathing? So late?'

'Peggy is helping me. Just like Kyi used to.'

She threw him a conciliatory smile. He nodded and withdrew. It appeared then that he had second thoughts, because immediately he popped his head around the door again.

'I will let you know my decision in the morning, Margaret.'

'William?'

He raised his eyebrows enquiringly.

'Did you strike the gong while you were downstairs?'

'As a matter of fact, I did. I was just thinking about – oh, all kinds of things, I suppose.'

'You are nostalgic.'

'Probably.'

'I am not nostalgic, William. Not in the least.'

'I realise that. We'll speak again in the morning, my dear.'

A darker rage built in her now, at his nerve in prolonging the thing, even though she had advised him to think about it. But if he had one cell of spontaneity in his being, surely he would have let the matter go tonight and come to a decision? But no, she was going to have to endure a night of it, waiting and wondering about whether or not she was entitled to learn something new, from prescribed textbooks, with examinations, and eventually a degree.

She slipped into the bath and began to soap her feet with a flannel, pressing it well between each of her toes. Peggy came in and busied herself folding towels for some moments.

'What was that song, earlier?' Margaret asked, humming a few bars.

'D'ye not know it? *My Lagan Love?*'

'I thought it sounded familiar, but I had forgotten it. Three years away but the moment I caught your voice it began to come back to me. Not the words, but the melody.'

Peggy knelt down and rinsed a soft blue flannel in the bathwater. She lifted a fresh bar of Rosewater-scented Castile soap, then pressed it to the cloth a few times before laying it on Margaret's back. Margaret moaned with pleasure, the fine skin drawn tight across her vertebrae as she leaned forward, exquisitely alive with sensation and relief as the day's toil and sweat was sluiced away. The melody rose to her throat and she hummed to herself, chin on knees as always. What a melancholy air, she thought, that caught the feeling of something being half-gained, but always lost.

'That's too sad a song for this late hour, Mrs,' Peggy said quietly, leaning with a little more vigour into Margaret's back, the facecloth moving deeper down her spine as she did so.

'It suits my mood,' came the reply.

'Ah now.'

The sweet odour of lathered soap filled the air, the water plinked softly. Farther down the landing a bedroom door clicked shut as William shut off the day.

Margaret suddenly turned around and looked at the maid, one hand gripping the side of the bath. There was an urgency in her expression. Peggy stopped what she was doing.

'What, Mrs?'

Margaret said nothing. She seemed to scrutinise Peggy's face very carefully, before settling on her grey eyes, which were open and honest.

'What is it?'

'Ah, Peggy, isn't life very complicated, even when we have all the things we want?'

'Indeed an it is, no doubt about that!'

'There is always something that eludes us. And rules to test.'

She reached up towards the maid, and catching her gently with her free arm drew her face close to her own. Slowly, she kissed her on one cheek then pushed her cautiously away again.

'There is always something,' Peggy echoed uneasily, blushing, touching her face as if it had been struck.

But Margaret turned to her again and, drawing the other woman close, now kissed her shyly on the mouth, then pushed back a long curl that had fallen across Peggy's face.

'There,' she said, blinking slowly, 'Perhaps I am breaking a rule of affection. I hope you do not object. It means nothing bad.'

'Of course not, Mrs. How could it be bad?' Peggy whispered, her eyebrows flickering down in puzzlement, her face now very ruddy.

She remained silent as she washed and rinsed, then began to hum the song again as the last of the soap rolled off and down into the water. In the bathroom window a lone moth danced against the pane, trying to escape to the moonlight.

'The thing is,' Margaret murmured, 'perhaps we're never as happy as we think we are, or as sad as we think we are either.'

FORTUNE ON A FAIR DAY
Monaghan, 1916

It seemed that fate had finally touched his shoulder, even if its timing was awry.

'What in Jaysus's name takes you over there?' his Uncle Jack snorted at the news. 'Just when your own country is close to getting what it wants.'

Jack leaned closer to the open-fronted range, a hunk of bread impaled on the end of a toasting fork. Although it was late April and mild, the kitchen still oozed waves of heat from the glowing coals. Uncle Jack's cronies had also assembled, as they often did just after the dinner. They waited and smoked as he prepared his own separate repast of toast and a boiled egg, on account of what he called his 'dropped stomach'.

'You need a kicked backside,' his uncle added as a final word.

Arthur did not reply. He had braced himself for such a response, but was not about to discuss the matter in the presence of Jack's loyal Greek Chorus. Half the family agreed with his decision to enlist with the Royal Irish

Fusiliers, while the other half grunted and pulled faces. As consumption had taken his mother the year before, he consoled himself in the knowledge that at least he did not have to face her, though he guessed she would not have opposed his decision, no more than his father. His father, while not exactly overjoyed, nonetheless stuck his hands deeper into his trouser pockets, frowned into the fireside and nodded his assent.

'There isn't much for you around here, son,' he remarked, 'though, as I've said before, I could take you on myself.'

'Have I disappointed you, Daddy?'

'No, son, you have not. Amn't I blessed with seven sons?'

His gentle father's occasionally hinted at hope was that he might join him in the family butchering business, that the words *John A. Duffy & Sons*, already emblazoned in gold lettering against the black enamelled shop front might finally mean something. Since Arthur was the first of seven sons, and had some misgivings about his filial shortcoming, he was relying on several of his brothers – on Simon, Francis, Celestine, Seamus, Kevin and Dermot – following their father into the business.

But at eighteen fate had called him and he wanted to serve something greater than their own small Irish troubles, which had kept people uneasy like a whinging child in the background of their days that they did not know quite how to help stand on its own two feet.

A week after he enlisted and told the family of his plans, he took a long walk out of the town. He needed to clear his head of the voices, opinions and clamour of their home on Dublin Street, where the cook and the laundry woman their father had employed since his wife's death were prone to voice opinions as diverse as the rising cost of meat, the language question or the war in Europe. Peggy, whose substantial rabbit stews and Sunday beef roasts, whose fragrant bowls of cabbage and sweet parsnip, massive pots of champ with little pools of melting butter, kept their bellies full, disagreed vehemently with Annie. Up to her elbows in the week's steaming sheets Annie was in no mood to concur with anything uttered by her kitchen companion. He was right to go, Peggy pronounced. He was a madman, Annie argued, dark curls stuck to her moist forehead as she pounded the sheets in the tub, then turned them over with the wooden tongs. Nothing good would come of it, she shouted for good measure, as if Peggy was slightly deaf.

In an effort to escape such conversational jousts, Arthur simply left the house. It was a Saturday, and his father could have done with help in the shop, but Arthur persuaded Francis to don the heavy white apron. His brother, being always the willing one in the family, sharpened his carving and cleaver knives and prepared to bone, carve, cut and tie the joints of meat that day. He would also have to go out on his bicycle and distribute the latest printed announcement that John A. Duffy wished to inform the nobility, gentry, farmers and townspeople of the arrival of a new consignment of best beef reared on the Barony of Larney and that excellent meat and prices were guaranteed to prevail.

There was no history of going to war in the family, no point to which he could cast his mind back and proudly witness men in uniform who had defended something they valued against a common enemy. A few families in the town had had members killed by the Boers, almost sixteen years before, and his father had occasionally mentioned an uncle of his who was in the Irish Republican Brotherhood during the failed 1867 Rebellion. After that, the uncle had left Ireland for America and they had not heard from him since. But otherwise Arthur had no knowledge of military achievement or excellence beyond what he had read about in books and there was no one to whom he could speak. Yet the voices of the recruiters had excited him. They seemed like the honourable characters in novels he had borrowed from the town library. From what they said, a fellow like him could rise through the ranks. He was strong and he was literate. He also knew how to horse ride, thanks to childhood summers as a stable boy for the Westenras, sometimes working with the estate trainer.

Now he was alone for a few hours. He left the town by the North Road and turned left up the hill. A train pulled out of the station and rumbled beneath the bridge as he passed. Steam rose between the green-painted iron railings and wrapped itself around his body for a moment before it evaporated and the train rattled and hissed along the track, north towards Belfast. He paused as it curved around a bend and eventually disappeared towards the bridge at Tullyherim. The blackthorn was in bloom everywhere and a light breeze sent the sweet blossoms in drifts onto the tracks. Here and there the bushes were pink-tinged so that they looked like pink, clotted cream. As he walked farther out the road and left the streets behind, the lime trees and beeches that draped themselves over the high garden walls of the larger houses in that part of the town were in half-bloom. Already, flies whizzed by like small pellets. A horse chestnut tree was in blossom and here the buzzing was intense as the insects staggered heavily in the air, then burrowed into the sweet candle flowers. Finally, Arthur reached a point on the road where, if one did not keep going straight, it branched off towards Armagh. He paused to admire a vast hill of ox-eye daisies, a golden saturation of light in the late afternoon, before deciding to walk straight for another half mile or so when he could turn left and begin a circular route that would bring him back into the town by the Infirmary Road.

As the quietness deepened, and there was nothing to hear – no cart, no horses, no human voice – he began to fret. He would have to see Molly Connolly before he left for war. He would have to explain things and hoped he might convince her once and for all that he believed he had no choice, that there was something in his blood that danced to make the world a better place. What she might not find so reasonable was that he wanted her to wait for him. It was six weeks since he had last seen her. On that occasion he had cycled to Augher so that he could see her in her parents' home, in the small but thriving public house they ran in the village. He arrived, tired and perspiring, his vest and shirt stuck to his back beneath the woollen jacket he had worn, his best. Her parents were not against him, for which he was relieved. Behind the public house lay the rest of the household, and a big kitchen through which a pet pig wandered, snuffling along, its bright eyes observing everything. Because Molly was fond of the pig, he kept his own counsel and made no comment.

Before that, he had met Molly on five occasions. The first was the previous autumn when he attended the Fair Day in his own town and spotted a slim girl with strawberry-blonde hair standing before a fortune teller. She was captivated, it seemed, as the canny gypsy read the palms of women, young and old. Tucked away from the main tussle of the beasts, in an archway beside a pawn shop, and despite the fact that the streets were a wet and slimed greenish brown on the day the cattle were marketed, all was clean where the fortune teller had set up her table.

'A penny for your thoughts,' Arthur had said shyly.

The girl whipped around and looked a little embarrassed.

'Money wouldn't buy them,' she said pertly, gathering herself and turning her gaze again towards the gypsy.

'I could tell your fortune quite easily,' he went on.

At this, the gypsy, who was attending to a middle-aged single woman, started slightly and flashed her eyes in his direction.

'Aren't you the great fella, so!' she scoffed gently. 'And I could tell *your* fortune, if you had the courage to hear it.'

Her spinster customer, who was leaning in intensely so as to catch every last syllable the brown-skinned fortune teller uttered, whirled around in annoyance at the interruption. She was hoping to hear of a dark and romantic stranger who would enter her life and transform it from its everyday misery of dashed hopes and the bodily frustrations that gnawed at her unrelentingly, which she could not discuss with anyone. She made an impatient tutting sound and turned back to the gypsy.

But Arthur ignored them both, transfixed by the girl. Her eyes, he noticed, were wide-set and grey, and there was a very small gap between her top teeth which made her seem mischievous. Since she did not respond to his teasing comment, and he desperately wanted her attention, he decided to try again.

'Yes, I could tell your fortune, if you'd let me.'

Now her face broke into a smile and for the first time she turned away from the gypsy and looked him up and down, her expression impish.

'Are you going to stand there all day with that silly smile on your *phisog*?'

'I could tell you that hundreds of men will love you but that only one will give you his heart entirely.'

Now she placed both hands on her hips and pursed her lips. 'If you carry on with that line of talk, I promise you won't be one of them.'

He felt very foolish. He heard the gypsy finish up with the spinster, telling her that she would have the life she deserved, which to his amazement pleased the woman, who walked away with a dreamy expression in her eyes and a smile playing at the corners of her lips. The gypsy then ushered the young girl forward. He watched.

'Can't you at least tell me your name before she begins?' he interrupted.

'Molly,' she hissed back over her shoulder.

The girl sat and ignored him. Straight away she crossed the gypsy's palm with a silver coin, then proffered her right hand. He was aware of the gypsy keeping an eye on him, but had no idea of her appraising thoughts. She had seen people coming and going all her life and had learned to read every anxiety and desire that afflicted the human condition. For, in her view, the human race was afflicted, even in its ecstasies, and nothing she could do or say would ever change that. From the set of him, and from the chancy way of his approach to the girl, she categorised him as a dreamer, one of the most afflicted cases she had met in a long time. Of all the categories of humans to whom calamities could fall, almost for no particular reason other than that the dreamer was in a certain place at a certain time, and usually not paying attention to what was practical and therefore important, this was the one category of person she tried to provide with honest advice. It was for their own protection. Even so, most of them never listened, but returned to her year after year, having ignored her advice and predictions, yet always believing in fresh possibilities, as is the nature of a dreamer. And who was she to reject the silver they never disputed?

She glanced at the girl's palm, while Arthur watched from behind. Her glance deepened to a study, as she examined the lines and mounds on the firm young hand. Then she sighed, shifting uncomfortably in her seat. She stared at Molly's hand again, without raising her eyes.

'What's wrong?' Molly asked.

'You could have a good future –' the gypsy began, then broke off.

'Could?'

'Hold your whisht, girl,' the gypsy snapped. 'I have something to consider.'

She raised her brown eyes to Arthur. He stared back at her with growing unease. Perhaps it was time to give up.

'Would you prefer – should I leave?' he asked politely.

'You can stay if you wish. It's up to her,' the woman replied, nodding to Molly.

At this, Molly stood up impatiently and shoved the chair back in against the small table.

'Well I have to say, you're some fortune teller! You tell me I *could* have a good future. Could is no use at all to me, and I'd like my money back if you don't mind. It's people with your kind of blather that are ruining our country, so Father says, and do you know something? I think he's right!'

The gypsy sat well back and took her ease, completely unruffled as she watched the girl. If anything, she appeared satisfied. Then she turned to Arthur.

'Can't you both see what's as clear as day to anyone but a *morán*? That the two of you have taken the fortune and are making it for yourselves before my eyes? Sure how can I work with her with the heat of your want at her shoulder like the demon lover?'

She watched as the pair of them began to argue, the girl blaming the boy for his interference and the boy trying to defend himself but not taking it at all seriously because he was so delighted to have this girl's attention all to himself. They moved off down the street, dodging the cattle and horses for sale, until they finally disappeared around a cluster of farmers deep in local gossip. One of them spat on his hand and smacked it strongly into another man's work-hardened paw. There was, the gypsy concluded yet again, no accounting for human nature and there was nothing she could do to deflect the path of love. Satisfied as she was, she also felt quite miserable. She could sense outcomes.

But Arthur was overjoyed. To his surprise, contrary though Molly was and easily annoyed, she nonetheless seemed content enough with his company. They spent the afternoon together. He bought her rose lemonade and a fruit scone at one of the stalls. They drifted through the crowds, ghostly yet never more fleshly, oblivious to the smell of animal ordure, blind to the hectoring men, ignorant of the passage of coins and notes from one hand to another. He told her about his father's butchering business and how it was expected that he would continue in the business, along with his brothers when they were old enough. But it did not interest him, he added cautiously.

'What do you want to do so?' Molly asked.

'I don't know. Something that matters, I suppose.'

At the end of a day in which time seemed to have unfurled like an eternal piece of string, without interruption, they agreed to write to one another.

The letters were brief, practical, always mentioning a time and a place for meeting, sometimes concluding with an endearment of some kind, mostly on Arthur's part. Gradually, through them, he eased his way towards the question of something more permanent, without being too explicit. Marriage was some way ahead.

Any time his father was taking the horse and cart to go the twenty-five miles or so to her village, Arthur made a point of accompanying him. The pattern after five meetings was to let her know in advance with a short note. After he returned home again in the evening when the day's business was over but also when he would have seen her, he knew he could expect a returning letter two days later. Peggy would tease him as she placed a piled dinner plate before him, saying that there was nothing like young love and his head was away with the fairies of late.

Dear Arthur,

Father doesn't object to our being so great with one another. So that's one thing you needn't worry yourself about. If it's alright with you, I may be able to get a lift to Monaghan the next Fair Day. I won't be having my fortune told though, and as you know, Arthur, we make our own fortunes although that gypsy woman moves around the counties of Monaghan and Tyrone all the time. She must know everybody's secrets and is surely rich by now. But I trust her to hold her tongue, otherwise the people would not keep visiting her. Well Arthur I must sign off, hoping this finds you well, as I am, Your Molly

He had kept her letters. There must have been ten at least, and he bundled them together with a piece of white string from the shop. He would not be writing to Molly about his enlisting. He had to see her. As it happened, the next Fair Day was in early May.

My dear Molly,
How are you? As you can imagine, I am eagerly looking forward to seeing you again. I am happy to note that you have found a way to get here for the next Fair Day, as I would dearly like to speak about a personal matter that concerns us both.
I await your reply,
Yours in tenderness,
Arthur

Being Molly, she did not reply but instead turned up on the day, knowing she would find him hovering in Church Square, a little down from the main frenzy of the Fair Day activity. She looked happy, Arthur thought, relief flooding through him as she approached. They stood and chatted for some time outside the railings of the Protestant church. They spoke of everything and nothing, they laughed a lot, as if life was a comedy. She seemed to like it when he told her jokes, which encouraged him to tell her even more. Her laughter rose on the air beside the church as if a great giddiness had overwhelmed her. Spontaneously she slipped her arm through his and began to guide him away and up the hill to the vicinity of the fair where there were sweet stalls and carpet salesmen down at the cleaner end of the street.

'Father will want to keep an eye on me, Arthur. He likes to know I'm in good company, which I am, of course, but that I have not disappeared.'

'Your father loves you for sure,' Arthur replied.

'He has never slapped me, though Mother didn't spare the rod when we were young!'

He gave an easy laugh. 'A case of spare the rod and spoil the child?'

She shook her head by way of reply, a frown making her fine eyebrows dip.

How would he tell her? How in heaven's name was he to break the news that he was leaving Ireland the following week to go to war with the British? It had been an impulsive decision, he knew, yet also the right one. It was fate, he was sure of it, something intended for him. He also knew he wanted to marry Molly, but not just yet. And it seemed that his feelings were reciprocated, that Molly Connolly saw herself linking his arm for many a year to come.

They strolled on towards the main thoroughfare, where drovers were still arriving with small herds and other men had already penned their animals.

'Molly, I have something to ask you,' he began hesitantly as they moved up the street towards the Market House.

Before she could respond, they both stopped. Men were gabbling furiously and not about the price of cattle. There was none of the sly and knowing rural badinage that characterised the marketing of beasts. Molly and Arthur advanced to the edge of a small crowd intent on listening to a newspaper account of some kind. The reader's voice quivered with indignation as he read how, one day before, fifteen Irishmen were executed by firing squad in Dublin. As he continued, the crowd grew silent, their faces sombre. Arthur caught Molly's hand and cradled it in both his, his confusion mounting. Oh God, he thought, now this. The man with the newspaper was reading what one member of the Irish Parliamentary Party had said in the House of Commons and how his impassioned words had shocked the House. He had spoken of the executed men not as murderers, but as insurgents who had fought a clean fight, a brave fight and only three thousand of them, ill-equipped against twenty thousand with machine guns and artillery.

Molly clutched at her throat as she listened.

'And to think we all thought they were a crowd of trouble makers!' she whispered.

'No. They were never that,' Arthur replied bitterly. Perhaps, in a perverse way, fate was not about to favour him after all. What he had heard had shocked him. For the first time, he began to question his own decision. And yet – surely it was an honourable thing for him to wish to fight against the Germans?

Again, he began to draw her back down the town. On the way he saw Uncle Jack coming up. When he spotted Arthur he pointed at him, then stopped and glared as if he was shaping up for an argument.

'You've heard then?'

'Aye.'

'It's a poor lookout when some of our own, who wanted nothing but freedom, who were prepared to do anything for it, are treated like criminals. Worse even. No trial nor nothing.'

'It's a shockin' thing,' Arthur agreed.

'You're coming to your senses then?'

Arthur said nothing. He did not wish to pursue this particular line of conversation in front of Molly. Miraculously, Uncle Jack had nothing more to communicate than a curt nod in Molly's direction before advising Arthur to look after that wee lassie no matter what else he might be thinking.

'What does he mean by that?' Molly asked, but Arthur just shook his head.

After he broke the news, they walked for hours. There was no convincing her, it seemed.

'I'm annoyed that you would even think of joining up, Arthur. Have you no desire for Ireland's own freedom? Have you not just heard your man reading the paper? We want to be free now. We can't stand by and let the English shoot our men like that!'

'Nobody gave a damn about them until this week.'

'Strong language like that doesn't make me afeard of you. That's as may be. But now the men are dead and we understand what their intentions were. That they were true-hearted and brave. How many of us can say that about ourselves?'

He did not know what to reply. What she said was true, but surely what he wanted might also be worth a hearing, only she could not see it that way.

'I had hoped – I had hoped you might wait for me, Molly. And I had hoped that I might be true-hearted and brave.'

'That is another matter, Arthur. You are going to war with the *English*.'

'But it's one of the ways to freedom! That Dillon man who spoke in the House of Commons has assured us that joining the British cause is the best way towards Home Rule. Surely you want Home Rule too? We can't all be like the insurgents, giving our blood, with the foolish people not fully behind us until it is too late!'

For the first time she seemed less certain of herself. They walked on, not holding hands, separate and more than cross with one another. They wandered far out into the countryside, following the course of the river Blackwater for some of the way. The air was loud with birdsong as they approached the river and slid down through the long grass and meadowsweet until they finally sat on the bank.

'If you want me to wait, I'll have to think about it,' she finally announced, glancing at him.

'So you'll permit me to go?'

'Is there any stopping men when they are determined to go to war?'

Again she was speaking the truth. She knew him well, even in so short a time. There was no stopping him and he would go.

'I will return, you know.'

'You might not. What about Gallipoli? Or don't they read the papers in your house?'

'I'm not going to Gallipoli. I'm headed for France and we'll sort out those Germans very quickly.'

'Well then ...'

'You trust me, don't you, Molly? I wouldn't spin you a yarn. I want only the truth. But there's this thing eats me – a need to do something – something that matters. It's Ireland I'm thinking of too, you know. Every Irishman who enlists is making his mark on our chance of Home Rule. I believe that. You should too.'

'As I said, Arthur, I will have to think about it, and without you telling me what I should think.'

It seemed that she had only half accepted his words, but in the end, they sat down in the grass and kissed. He tried to undo her blouse but she firmly caught his hand and stopped him. Her cheeks were flushed, her grey eyes bright. She sat up and wrapped her arms around her knees and faced the river.

'Look, a kingfisher!'

He propped himself on one elbow, but it was too late. She had caught the halcyon flash as he was looking skywards, tracing cloud shapes as he absorbed the delight of her kisses.

She would think about waiting for him, she had said. And he would be home again in less than a year, victorious with the rest of his battalion, so it was not so much to ask of a girl. Surely she would wait and not go off with somebody else. She was not the kind of girl who fell easily into the arms of every man who came her way. He imagined that she loved him greatly, as he did her, and if two people were in love there could be no impediment.

'So.'

He waited as she prepared to speak.

'So you'll be seeing the fields of France, in your fine uniform.'

'I will.'

'Even with the awful things we heard today, I'm coming to believe that your cause is a just cause too, because otherwise it wouldn't interest the likes of you.'

She fell silent, before finally turning towards him again.

'I wish you weren't going away, but I suppose I'll see you again, Arthur?'

At this, he caught her by the waist and drew her close again.

'You *will*. I promise!'

'I have to admit I always liked the cut of a man in uniform,' she giggled.

'Did you now, Molly Connolly? Well then, you shall see one sooner than you imagine, heading off to war!'

'And when you come home from France, we'll be married.'

'And you will live with me in Monaghan, where we will have children and be very happy.'

At this she hesitated. Turning, she tapped him on the chest with one finger.

'Will I now? My father has set aside a wee bit of ground out the country that would be perfect for our house. You might think of that too. Could you see yourself in Augher?'

To reply to that seemed irrelevant just then. He had never considered living anyplace else but his own town, having assumed that the woman he would wed would be happy to join him there. So, instead, he wrestled her in some more tomfoolery, and when the kissing resumed, this time she did not catch his wrist so firmly or push him away.

Dusk was falling when they walked back to the town. Bats pipped and wheeled beneath darkening trees. He told her another joke. She laughed at it, her pink mouth widening to a mischievous smile, her eyes dancing. She could not wait to see him in uniform, she said.

THE BLACK CHURCH
Dublin, 24 April 1916

Ann Jane wiggled the doll's head, her two fingers lodged within the empty interior. She held up her hand and stared at the eyes. They flapped open as she bent her fingers slightly, then snapped shut again when she tilted her hand in the other direction. Her mother had gone down to Moore Street for a few herrings, leaving Ann Jane in charge of the Ba.

The Ba dragged herself along the floor on her bare bum. She was tethered around the waist with a thin leather leash which stretched to the leg of the table, around which it was knotted. She had a runny nose and a bad cold. Even so, she cooed pleasantly to herself, making swipes at Ann Jane, whom she couldn't quite reach. Her chubby fingers stretched out again and again, as she grunted. Every so often the Ba gave a yowl of frustration. She would push herself forward, propping herself on both arms then arduously try to get her legs to lever her upright. But much as she wanted to she couldn't walk yet.

Ann Jane ignored the Ba, glad of the relative quiet in the room. Her three brothers were below on the street. She knew that because, even three floors up, she recognised the gravelly shouts of the twins – Jimmy and Seán – and even the lighter, asthmatic rasp of Tomás. All three were older than Ann Jane.

She sighed and addressed the doll's head. 'If it wasn't for me you wouldn't be here, Belinda. You should be grateful I saved you from *Hell!*' she announced, giving the head a vigorous shake. She went on to describe the fire in the toyshop and what she saw the evening when she and Ma were on their way back from St Francis Xavier's Hall.

Ma used to bring Ann Jane to the moral meetings, even though, as she would tell her daughter, it was really Da who should be going to them. They had heard Fr Cullen talk about drink and depravity. His recommendations for avoiding drink and depravity had something to do with devotion to the Sacred Heart of Jesus, which would help even someone like Da to give up his ways and stop spending money they didn't have on porter and whiskey.

'So there we were, Belinda – Ma and me walking along after all the talk about the bad people drinking, when all of a sudden there's a WHOOSH …'

She paused for effect and brought the doll's face quite close to her own, as if daring Belinda to contradict her. Her voice dropped menacingly. With every detail she shook Belinda's head even more, reminding her yet again of her good fortune in escaping death by fire.

Ma and Ann Jane had witnessed it all. Mr Morosini's toyshop had been embroiled and the whole premises destroyed. They had stopped to join the crowd of gawkers. They watched as a line was organised and firemen approached while buckets of water were launched into the air, in through the windows from which the glass had exploded, such was the terrible heat within. The street was roasting hot, the flames yellow and purple, sometimes green and blue, Ann Jane noted, but even worse was the violent sound from within.

Pop! Pop! Pop! She strained her ears. There it was again. *Pop! Pop-pop-pop-pop-pop-pop! Rata-tata-tata-tata! Pop-pop-pop!* Inside Mr Morosini's, lovely things were exploding or melting, or both, and the sound of the deaths of his dolls and teddies entered Ann Jane's ears like hot, painful needles.

'Ma,' she wailed, 'Mr Morosini's dollies are burning!'

She pitied the shop owner whose dolls were surely like his children, just as the one doll Ann Jane had was as real as the Ba, only better, because she never cried and was only slightly smelly.

For several years now she had pressed her face and nose up close to Mr Morosini's toyshop window. Sometimes she had wandered inside on her way home from school but the Italian had never encouraged her to dally. He would smile and gesture at his dolls and teddies, as if showing her his pride and joy, but then he would wag his forefinger at Ann Jane too. She disliked wagging fingers and shaking heads which characterised most interaction between older people and children. So she mostly stared in through the window, selecting the doll she would like best if God was as powerful as he was supposed to be and could grant your heart's desire.

Her heart's desire was for the dark-haired, ringleted doll called Prima Donna. Nobody had bought her. She sat, big and beautiful, on the middle shelf behind Mr Morosini's counter, surrounded by lesser dolls who came and went and were regularly replaced. But the Prima Donna's cheeks were peachy-pink, the rest of her face creamy, lips a cherry red, eyebrows delicate and her eyes the sweetest brown Ann Jane had ever seen. Once she asked Mr Morosini if the Prima Donna's eyelids opened and closed. In reply he had taken the doll from the shelf and perched her on the counter in front of Ann Jane. Gently he tilted Prima Donna backwards and her eyes snapped shut in deepest sleep. Ann Jane clapped her hands at this. Then he tilted Prima Donna forwards and her eyes were suddenly wide open, staring straight at Ann Jane.

On the night of the fire Ann Jane knew that the Prima Donna had also died, her lace and satin ruffles dissolved, her body streaming a fiery lava that joined the rest of the dying dolls as they flowed, melted in death's hot river. There was one more *Pop!* though, and something shot from the blazing premises and landed, smoking but not on fire, not far from Ma's feet. The other onlookers shifted, murmuring in surprise. Ann Jane made to run forward but Ma restrained her.

'Don't touch. It might burn you.'

'But Ma!'

'I said wait.'

Ma's hazel eyes observed the object for a moment, then she let go of Ann Jane's hand.

'Just be careful.'

Ann Jane hunkered down and poked at it with her forefinger. It was a doll's head. Not the Prima Donna's head, but one who had once been a Goldilocks and was now a little untidy looking. Her hair had not been entirely burned off. Ann Jane turned it carefully in both hands. In fact the hair on the top of her head was untouched and only the long ringlets that would have hung down her back seemed to have been obliterated in the inferno. If Ma would trim the side curls the doll's head would be nice enough.

She called her Belinda. That night Da came home in good spirits and promised to make a raggedy body to fit Belinda's head and Ma promised to sew up some raggedy legs and arms. Her father's hands and face were filthy with coal dust; even between his teeth showed signs of coal. He had come from the docks with a hessian bag of lumps gathered along the road, between tram tracks, on the quays. He was sweating hard.

'We can blaze away for a few nights anyway if the weather turns cold,' he said with a smile, winking at Ma.

'I don't suppose you found anything to eat?' Ma stared at him with big eyes.

He shook his head slowly.

'Well there's nothing here, only what'd feed a mouse!' she snapped, throwing her hands up, then lowering them as quickly to her apron. Quickly she raised the apron to her face and moaned softly into it.

'Me belly's aching, that's the God's honest truth ...'

All their bellies were aching. Ann Jane's belly bubbled, churned and twisted within her almost every day. She had reached a point where at times all she ever thought about was eating. As she and Belinda trailed along Sackville Street, or down Talbot Street, she rarely missed an opportunity to stare at the contents of the sweet shop windows. Her favourite was Kennedy's Bakery in Great Britain Street. She would stand outside it quite deliberately, just to smell the ooze of heat and yeast that wafted from the doorway as women shoppers passed in and out. Her eyes lit greedily on their square-wrapped boxes, in which nestled cakes and buns. Sometimes she fancied that even the smell of these delicious things was nourishment, could fill her up for an hour or two, to carry her as far as break-time at school. The nuns gave out batch loaf and jam at break to anyone who wanted it, with girls who spoke the best Irish getting slightly thicker slices, sometimes with country butter from the father of one of the young novices. For that reason Ann Jane was learning Irish very quickly.

In recent weeks the confectionary and bakery windows had gradually filled with Easter eggs – tantalising ovals in various sizes. Kennedy's had also added chocolate eggs to its usual stock of bread and buns. She watched one day as a young man with protruding ears carefully placed an enormous egg right in the centre of the window, where it was surrounded, as if by admirers, by smaller eggs of various sizes. It was iced in scrolls of pink, blue and yellow, the words *Happy Easter 1916* done in white. The young man paused as he settled the egg, checking that his handiwork was stable on its supporting silvery stand, then glanced at Ann Jane. As usual, like many adults, he winked at her. She gave a small smile by way of response. It was beyond her why people felt the need to wink at childer like herself. It didn't change anything, although sometimes there was forgiveness in it, as if they, the childer, were not doing anything wrong after all. So often they were in the wrong and a wink, it was understood, conveyed an impression of kindness. After the young man had retreated into the shop she pressed her nose close to the window and peered in. Now the sweet scent of chocolate that lingered in the air from the half-open doorway contended with the yeasts and cooking odours she normally enjoyed.

'Do you want to come in?' a voice suddenly enquired.

She whirled around. It was the fellow with the big ears. She nodded, her eyes darting instinctively from ear to ear. One of them was slightly closer to the side of his head than the other, but it made little difference to the overall effect.

'Don't be shy,' he urged, holding open the door for her. As he did so a hurrying, plump woman in a feathered hat wiggled around Ann Jane, brushing so close that the hard fabric of her mustard-yellow sleeve grazed her cheek. Ann Jane touched her face automatically and followed the man inside.

All was calm and orderly. For a moment the odour of baking and sweetness almost overwhelmed her and she hooked her fingers to the edge of the big counter, to steady herself.

'You'd like some chocolate, wouldn't you?'

'Yes please, mister.'

He reached beneath the counter and rummaged around before lifting up a white paper bag.

'We make mistakes in this place,' he confided. 'The chocolate breaks. Or the boss doesn't like the mix. This batch, for example,' he thrust a bag across the counter, 'is too sweet. So His Nibs says. I don't agree but I can't say as much.'

He shook his head and wiggled his eyebrows up and down.

'Why don't you tell him we like sweet things in Ireland?' Ann Jane asked cautiously.

The man regarded her soberly for a moment. 'Little Miss, I've told him once, but he doesn't listen. Since he's been to France, you see, he's been trying to convert his customers to bitter chocolate.'

Ann Jane wrinkled her nose at the thought. The man pushed the bag towards her again, nodding. She felt her heart flutter as she reached forward to grasp it. It was almost as good as the day Da came home with five pounds ten shillings he'd won on a horse, when her heart had also fluttered and danced. Immediately, she ripped open the bag. There must have been nearly a pound of broken chocolate pieces.

'Now you'll be a good girl and not forget to share it?'

'Yes, mister,' she replied a little uncertainly.

'We should share everything, you know,' he added, but his eyes gleamed with mischief.

'Yes, mister.'

'Especially as we grow older. What age are you?'

'Ten and a half.'

He gave a light laugh. 'You won't be playing with that doll's head for much longer then, will you?'

That was a strange thing to say, she thought, as she drifted slowly up Granby Street, munching and sucking. It was the most wonderful chocolate, silky and sweet as it dissolved around her teeth. At first she had gulped it down, but now, as her stomach filled, she could afford to slow up. Besides, she would have to keep a few pieces for the Ba. The boys were not getting any because they had not shared the sticks of Peggy's Leg that one of them had stolen from a Belvedere boy on his way home from school the previous year.

Easter, she imagined, would be like every other Easter she remembered, which were not very many, but were nevertheless marked by sameness and an absence of celebration. There would be early Mass, of course, with Ma and the Ba and her brothers. Ma liked to talk about how the sun danced for sheer joy on the Dublin hills at Easter, on account of the Resurrection of Our Lord. It was understood by the children that Da might or might not attend Mass, depending on his state of health.

And it was as she had anticipated. Although not so hungry because they had had a broth of oxtail, carrots and barley in the middle of the day, followed by a strawberry jelly dessert from a package which one of the boys said was just lying on the street the day before, Easter was in every other respect unremarkable. Neither Ma nor Da had asked questions about the jelly and the whole family had enjoyed it, scooping precious spoonfuls from the blue delph basin in which it had been made. That afternoon, because of their meal, the room smelt different – there was saltiness and beefiness in the air as well as a hint of sweet strawberry. Everybody was in good humour, although the Ba kept coughing.

Even so, boredom set in very quickly after dinner and Ann Jane left the flat to wander the streets. As usual Belinda's head was fixed to her fingers, so that she could conduct a conversation should she wish to.

'So, Belinda, today we're going to the Black Church,' she announced quietly, crossing the street towards St Mary's Place.

She had decided to make the trip having heard Mrs Anderson in the room above theirs talking to Ma the previous week about that church and how if you walked three times anti-clockwise around it at midnight you could summon the Devil. Why anyone would want to summon the Devil at midnight or any other time was beyond her, but Ann Jane did not fear this entity because Ma had laughed softly at the notion and, later that day when Ann Jane had enquired, Da had told her the only devils were the ones with flesh and blood who'd take the last crumb from a person's mouth if they could. Vicious scroungers like Mr Murphy and the like who opposed working men joining the union.

Nevertheless the idea amused her. Because it was Easter Sunday, and therefore a very holy day, she decided to walk three times around the Black Church bearing in mind that it was not midnight. When she had done it she would certainly inform Mrs Anderson at the first opportunity. She crossed the street, glanced up at the church at the same time as she whispered in Belinda's pinkish left ear. What she whispered were not actual words, so much as half-formed lisps of intimacy and apprehension. She wanted to convince Belinda that this was an adventure worth having and that they would walk three times around and taunt the Devil, who could not appear even if he wanted to, because it was not midnight.

The church loomed sinisterly ahead, spikey-pinnacled and dark against the clear sky.

'So, Belinda, are you ready?'

Belinda's head nodded in response. The entire street was deserted. In the distance Ann Jane could hear the sounds of horses pulling carts, then the rumbling cartwheels themselves describing the passage of the afternoon. She also heard the shouts and cries of children. Some people had lit their fires, and already the air was trailing smoke with a grey-flannel haze hovering over certain buildings. But the sky was like a jewel and the day sunny. The Devil could never appear to anyone at such times. He represented darkness, fire and brimstone and the things the priests spoke of up at St Francis Xavier.

Ann Jane clutched Belinda to her chest as she planted her foot firmly to the right of the church door. She glanced once more over her shoulder and, as she sucked her small mouth in tight at the sight of the tall oval of the entrance, dimples appeared on her cheeks. She continued purposefully around the side of the church at an unvarying pace. When she had completed three circles of the building she stopped exactly where she had begun.

'Now, Belinda. Let's wait.'

Ann Jane regarded the high entrance, the arch and spike and interleaved stone that cradled the doorway. If he was going to appear it would be like a fizz of smoke or mist. He would not descend from the archway. He would arise from below, moiling his way into her vision so that she would sense him even before she saw him, swirling up from beneath the dungeon-like cellar grid at the base of the church walls. She waited, feeling more satisfied by the second, as the moment expanded and there was no defining darkness, no spectre to obliterate her and the city around her.

'See Belinda?' She turned Belinda's face towards her own. 'Told you, didn't I? Nothing to worry about! Now we must go home because Ma will be wondering where we are.'

Ann Jane woke on Easter Monday to another bright day. Da had already left. Although he could not go to the races at Fairyhouse he wanted to be on the streets, to catch all the gossip as word came of winning horses. Ma did not get up at all, but clung to the Ba and stayed in the horsehair bed behind the dark green curtain that divided the room at night. Ann Jane could hear the Ba gurgling and snuffling. Her cold had become a thick and musical cough, like pipes playing out of tune as her small chest attempted to breathe.

Ann Jane moved quietly from her own tumbled bedding on the floor. Her brothers lay in deepest sleep. Jimmy's mouth was wide open and a trail of saliva drooled onto the flour sacking beneath his head. Seán and Tomás were silent, their chests rising and falling gently. Seán's browny fists, his black little fingernails, gripped the two woollen blankets that covered his body, as if in sleep he had to be on his guard.

She would go to Mrs Anderson and see if she was up. Perhaps she would have a slice of bread or some tea. She pressed hard at the skirt of her dress, as if to smooth the creases, before pulling at her hair so that it was not hanging over her eyes. Grownups disliked hair falling into eyes and across noses. They had a habit of pushing it back, and not always gently, so that they could see you. Then they would study you as if there was something written in your eyes worth reading. Mrs Anderson was like that.

But Mrs Anderson was not up or else she had gone out. It was a quarter to twelve, almost midday. Just as Ann Jane was making her way down the long stairs, she heard a sound. It was not the usual creaks and dull thuds that were part of the acoustics of the big house in which the different families lived. There was no tin-whistle to be heard from the O'Flaherty's, nor was it the deep voice of Mr Toolan as he clobbered his wife; nor was it the secret silence – in itself a sound – that enveloped the floor on which the young Mr and Mrs Harry Dunne lived when they closed their door and shut out the world. So far, they had no childer, and Ann Jane knew they were happy, even though she had heard Mrs Anderson once remark that it was high time they had a little one to look after to take them down out of the clouds. On the one occasion she had glimpsed inside their tidy little room, there were no clouds to be seen, nor buffeting out from between the cracks in their door. The sound did not emanate from any of the usual sources. She looked around her. Above, the ceiling plaster was crumbling, the coving also breaking up with dampness. It was a sound from outside their world, one that she could not quite define, because it was not properly within her hearing so much as in her sense of something about to happen. It was a warning, she decided.

Out on the street, with Belinda on her fingers, she wandered to the bottom of North Great George's Street, turned right along Great Britain Street and found herself at the top of Sackville Street. From where she stood there was a new busyness and tension in the air which made her stop in her tracks. Her eyes were drawn to the one building that stood like a fortress on the street, the place Ma had told her to avoid at night because of the women who hung around beneath the portico. Around the GPO people were clustered in groups, heads moving intently as they turned to one another. Crowds milled further out on the street, gazing at the portico of the building as if something unusual was occurring. People were running. She whirled her head around. From behind, a group of lancers on horses proceeded steadily down the street in the direction of the post office. She pressed her body against the wooden frame of a shop doorway and shrank back as the men then charged until they drew level with the GPO. Ann Jane's hands flew to her ears at the guns fired and split the air. Belinda fell to the ground. Ann Jane dropped to her knees and quickly scooped up her doll again. Almost as quickly the horsemen galloped back up the street, the people shouting after them. A woman screamed. Not so far from where she stood someone cursed. Her entire body trembled, her heart like a struck anvil, relentless in her chest as she peeked around the doorway again.

'Ah Jaysus, he's down!' someone called out.

At this, she sank to her knees and hunched up very small. Something terrible was happening. It was the Devil's revenge, for not being called at midnight, for having been fooled with in the middle of an Easter

Sunday, God's holiest day. Ann Jane did not know how long she stayed there, watching from her position close to the ground. All she knew was that the sun had almost disappeared and the street lights had begun to glimmer. What was she waiting for when Hell seemed to be rising around them on the streets? Clutching Belinda tightly to her chest she lisped and whispered, soothing herself as the *pop-pop-pop!* she'd heard not so long ago from Mr Morosini's shop again filled the air. There would be fire, she knew, and brimstone, which was apparently worse and instead of dolls' heads popping there would be devilish attempts to take the humans away from their innocent days with their hungry bellies. *Pop-pop-pop-pop!* She listened again and crouched on her hunkers for a long time. When it was completely dark she was still there with Belinda. She felt quite cold. The Devil himself had descended in their midst and it was entirely her fault. Because she had walked anti-clockwise around the Black Church, he had come up from Hell to possess the biggest building on Sackville Street, had driven the men and women in uniforms to rush inside and smash everything and the whole place would soon be blazing with demons.

But then she stirred. Her eyes tried to focus. Could it be? She snapped her eyes shut, as one of Mr Morosini's dolls might do, in case what she saw was not real, then as quickly snapped them open. It *was* real. Slowly she pushed herself to her feet, shaking her right foot which had gone numb. There was Mrs Anderson pushing a pram towards the conflagration, face flushed and happy. How peculiar, Ann Jane thought, to be pushing an empty pram so happily down the street, when Mrs Anderson's children were all grown and surely the shops were closed and there would be broken glass every place. But Mrs Anderson had spotted her and paused, holding the pram with one hand and placing the other one on her hip. She was still wearing her everyday apron, although a red felt hat was perched jauntily on her head.

'Child! *What* are you doing here?'

Ann Jane shook her head, as if warning Mrs Anderson to stay away. There was too much danger.

'Child, do you hear me? What are you doing, Ann Jane Gleeson, when the city is in uproar? Are you light-headed?'

She was light-headed. How correctly Mrs Anderson had observed that. She was light-headed with fear, not hunger. The woman approached her then, pulling the pram behind her and stuck out her left hand in Ann Jane's direction.

'You'd be better off with me, my angel,' she said firmly, catching the child by the elbow and drawing her towards her.

Ann Jane did not resist. Perhaps Mrs Anderson was right. Perhaps the thing to do was to walk alongside her as she made her way bravely down the street in the darkness of night with the pram. She might even pretend to be Mrs Anderson's daughter and she would be safe.

They approached a shop window in which the glass had been smashed and splintered. People crowded in, stepping over one another, jostling and pushing such was the rush. There was bread, criss-crossed and plaited, and bursting, shiny-crusted loaves scored with a knife, and there were cakes and sweets, and more chocolate than Ann Jane could ever have imagined as they followed the crowd inside. There was no fire or brimstone, merely glass to be avoided, and at last, fresh, sweet offerings on an altar of plenty.

'There you are, child. Sure don't you like fairy cakes too? Of course you do, of course you do …'

THE UNCHOSEN
Kilmainham Gaol, Dublin, May 1916

The cold in the East Wing puts paid to notions of sleep. No matter which way Dermot arranges his body, the biting teeth of the night chill gnaw his feet, numbing his toes and causing the muscles to cramp every so often. He has just fallen back onto his bunk after the latest cramp during which he was forced to stand and massage the arch of his right foot for a few moments before the muscles yielded. For what must be the tenth time he drags the blanket up over his head and breathes out hard so as to create a warm air tunnel that will penetrate down his legs towards his stiff and clammy feet.

Sleep is the least of his worries. Oblivion would be wonderful but it will never be his unless they decide to shoot him. A different oblivion. Not for the first time he grinds his fist against his teeth to stifle despair and the need to cry out in some manner. But tonight all is fairly silent in the gaol. There is a sense of anticipation, of dread, but also – he imagines – a sense of the inevitable. It pulls like a taut, thick rope drawn through the minds of all the separated men in their solitary cells, through the minds of their gaolers too, and with each passing minute that rope tightens and the anchor of the ship of death is already being raised.

Eventually, exasperated by the still-cool, now muggy air beneath the blanket Dermot gives up attempting to warm his body and sits up again. As he exhales, the cell is so cold and damp that even in the dark he can sense his own breath, its moisture clinging to his face, attaching itself to his cheeks like a spectre determined to enter his body. He fumbles with the matchbox and eventually manages to scratch a match to life. Even the sudden burst of heat affects him and for a moment he is tempted to hold it against his other hand to luxuriate in the brief squib of sensation. In the end, though, he lights the single candle and watches as it sputters, hisses and eventually settles in an uneven and shadowy glow.

He feels privileged to have lived so close to extremes. The molten glass of the huge, burning shop windows, the bombs rising like fireworks from the top of the General Post Office, the stifling, almost suffocating heat that eventually the men had to flee as the place collapsed around them. And now this. There were other extremes too, he reminds himself, to do with sides and decisions and whether one was cool and contingent regarding the rebellion or whether one cut one's own veins to let blood – drenched in love of nation and the chance of a future – flow into the dust of the streets if necessary.

He remains sitting with the blanket. This way he can double it slightly, increasing the possibilities of wan heat, legs tucked beneath. At his request they allowed him several sheets of paper and a pencil. For the fourth night he realises that, of all things, he wants to draw. On the other occasions he has sketched from memory images of his home in Kildare – the kitchen with its roaring fire, the shop crowded with articles of hardware, the long village street leading to the Carton Estate with its avenue of sweet lime trees, used by servant girls and boys for almost two hundred years. He holds up one of the thin pages he has already drawn on and scrutinises it by candlelight. It is the preliminary route to the stately home, a perfectly-straight demesne avenue that vanishes to a pinprick perspective where the double line of trees finish and the iron gate separates the land and its impregnable walls from the village. The sprawling-winged house with its Georgian section is nowhere to be seen, but the comings and goings of its occupants dominated village life for almost three centuries. There is Carton at one end and Maynooth seminary at the other with the ordinary people sandwiched between the high and mighty in two manifestations, often servants to both. His own family has served neither, having run their own shop already for fifty years. His father, moreover, owned twenty acres of the best-drained Kildare land not too far from the village.

In the dim light he begins to stroke the pencil on paper. He has no clue as to what he might draw other than to follow the compulsion itself. He exclaims to himself softly that he should be thinking of drawing on *this* May night, when so much is at stake. But his mind is frantic. There is, moreover, the question of his pain and of distracting himself from it as much as from the cold. A laceration on his left shoulder is slow to heal, the throb of it increasing marginally with each slow heartbeat, then relenting again. It must be infected. He wonders vaguely what his chances of securing medical aid will be. One of the guards has promised a doctor, which is how he guesses he is not to be executed.

But he cannot recall any image that appeals to him. He thinks back to the recent days in the GPO, which were not at all what he had anticipated after the one hundred and fifty or so men charged in that morning. But if he were to portray a truthful image? He could hardly capture that which mirrored the brazen disrespect of some of the customers as he and others vaulted across the public counters and shouted 'hands up!' No, not being taken seriously was not how they should be remembered in times to come. One woman even smirked at him, her eyebrows raised superciliously as he waved a gun in her face, advising her to get out. *For heaven's sake, what are you playing at?* she enquired archly. It took Connolly firing in the air to show her and her like that the men were deadly earnest and that this was full military action. Then they jumped to it. Yet even after the evacuation some of the fools continued to peer in through the windows as if the Volunteers were actors on a stage and they outside the gawking audience. But after that it settled and they found a routine which befitted their station and intention. The days passed. They held position and managed to break through to premises on the surrounding streets until they commanded the city centre. Or so it seemed.

Perhaps he can create a reflection of that breaking through of wall on wall, he thinks now, something to bring him back in contact with the wonderful sense of something changing, the fragmented birth of the new, driven by the smallest of groupings, and now half-aborted as far as he could see by forces so much greater and more powerfully equipped than they had ever been.

No, there was no point in drawing that, he concludes. There is nothing for it but to portray the damn cell. He regards the claustrophobic narrowness, the festering damp block walls, the stone-flagged floor. The doorway is set in a low arch, matched by the low arch of the ceiling above him. Thanks to that ceiling his sense of claustrophobia is not as pronounced as it might have been.

Dermot hunches over the page. It is a poor-quality notepaper, more suited for letter-writing or basic book-keeping, but it will have to do. The candle hisses and, although there is no draught that he is aware of in the seeping cold, the flame wavers as if blown gently by an invisible presence. He looks up to see the source of the air and even holds up his right hand on the other side of the candle but he can feel nothing. The pencil is poised between his fingers and thumb. Quickly, barely glancing up again to check the perspective, he starts to sketch the prison cell, walls, doorway, the arched ceiling, then the block work itself. He works in quick, straight strokes, then creates shade and the darkest recesses by hatching and cross-hatching, again in short, straight lines. Occasionally he stops to scrutinise his handiwork. It is just a cell, with no one in it. The miserable cell is what he seeks to capture. The light is dim but, even so, he can see that the image is an accurate one. Does it embody the full torment of his hell?

Somewhere farther along the corridor a door squeals open and he hears voices, followed by a female one. It is Grace, he thinks, surely that is she, now with Plunkett for their pathetic allotted time as husband and wife. Suddenly his own drawing sickens him. He flings it aside and it drifts to the floor. Some secondary impulse makes him bend and retrieve it though. He will leave nothing of himself in this place regardless of what they do with him. The paper is shoved in his right-hand pocket and he sits down heavily again.

As far as he knows Plunkett is to be shot in the morning, along with the others. Even if he were not in the gaol he is not in good health, the poor devil, with his tubercular throat and his bandage. He wonders if Plunkett's poetry is helping him now, the way his pencil has occasionally tamped down the worst of his terrors. Has Grace married him out of mercy at this stage? Of course not, he reprimands himself: they were engaged to be wed. And one night with a loved one can equal an eternity of bliss, except that this will not even be a night. They are getting ten minutes.

He hears the bastard outside Plunkett's cell counting down the minutes, literally, as the couple make the most of their time together. How passionate they must be, to withstand such callousness incised with the precision of a silversmith's tool – except this is no craftsman, but a demon of the administration. He longs to be part of such passion, part of the brave, hopeless courage that inspires the lovers at this late hour.

Apart from the guard's voice, all is quiet. They are together in a cell as narrow and chilling as his. They are man and wife and, regardless of his fate she will have been and will always be his wife. Plunkett, illness and all, could be said to be a fortunate man. He is beloved of a good woman. He wonders if they will dare embrace or kiss. Most likely, he thinks. After all when a man is going to his death ... But beyond that he cannot think. It is too awful to contemplate. This is not the outcome Plunkett's mother would have imagined for him as an infant, any more than his own parents would have been prescient enough to see him here locked up with his companions and counting down the hours.

He is grateful to the priests who have come and heard confessions and carried notes and letters. Fr Aloysius was with him three days before, offering to get word to his family in Maynooth. His presence made Dermot briefly peaceful and he was able to forgive himself for a while. But Aloysius will witness much more, he reasons; his duties do not begin and end in the cells because his strength and gentle ear, his keen care, will have to carry many of them forward.

Some time later a cell door is ripped open again and he hears a woman's footsteps. She is leaving. It is all so quick and hushed. There is not so much as a whisper or a cry from Plunkett's new wife, so far as he can make out. In an effort to see up to the right on the dank landing he presses his nose close to the small grid on his cell door. But his vision yields nothing. Only his ears follow her footsteps which are rapid and light. He imagines Plunkett's state of mind while realising he cannot remotely do so. If it were he? He would probably be hammering the cell door with his fists, kicking it with his feet in his rage and despair. But Plunkett has obviously moved to some higher plane, when such raw emotions are no longer of use and the body has no call for them. Perhaps there comes a stage where it really is possible to be reconciled and perhaps that is why they have chosen Plunkett as well as the others. They were always reconciled to their fate; they cared nothing for their lives so long as they succeed in achieving their end. Unlike him who does not believe in blood sacrifice. Not all the men do.

If it hadn't been for a chance conversation with a big-eared fellow in the bakery on Great Britain Street, who spoke with such conviction about the necessity of joining the Volunteers, he might never have been there on Easter Monday. He is the sort of man who can see both sides of an argument and find goodness in each. That is his problem. The others have always been quite clear-cut about their goals – rational, to be sure, but hot-blooded with poetry and ideals – but he could have been convinced either way. The politician Redmond's vision had seemed more than adequate, and armed force had never worked before. Defeat followed defeat, betrayal followed betrayal on down the centuries. They were a humiliated people, embodying what happens when people resist, and resist only to be flattened to the ground again and humiliated some more for good measure. So it was not unreasonable for him to think that Redmond's ideas might work. Reason. Working with the British rather than against them. But once he joined the Volunteers that also seemed the correct thing to do, its appeal quickly overtaking the quieter rationale of his previous views. Suddenly Ireland's need seemed so great that it was blindingly obvious even to him that something dramatic and untoward would have to occur if anything were to change.

That he is not to be one of the executed is almost a disappointment. After all he too had fought on the day; he was with them, heart, mind, body, blood. He had even brought provisions in advance from the shop in his own village. Tinned food, bread and milk, fresh ham to keep them going during the week they were holed up and the city outside took its time in springing forward to join the resistance.

But apparently his presence and activity have not been regarded as threatening enough despite the fact that he was there. Death awaits some of the others and fate has taken a baffling hand as he is condemned to wait and listen to the passing of their final hours. *God help them*, he prays every so often. *And God help poor Plunkett.*

In the roundups the lancers were rough and violent. There would be no mercy shown, it seemed.

He looks to the small window high up in the cell and catches sight of a few stars, the same stars that people out in the city can see should they chance to look up, the same stars that hover over his own county this night. Eventually from sheer exhaustion he leans in against the wall in a half-sitting position, the blanket wrapped tightly around him, and dozes off. The pencil he drew with earlier lies at an angle on the stone floor. He no longer cares whether he has a pencil or not. The drawing can go to hell. His own life is not worth recording since he has failed to be passionate and selfless enough to want to spill his own blood. Somehow he dozes off.

Later – it must be much later because he can hear the first birdsong and the sky is brightening – he is awoken by a racket from along the landing. Doors are being thrown open, voices clear and matter-of-fact. There is nothing unruly about this awakening. It is entirely planned that what is about to occur cannot be witnessed in broad daylight. It is to be a dawn execution in the central courtyard.

They care little or nothing for their lives – that much was always clear to him. He had tried to be as they were and now he feels cowardly, inadequate. Would he wish to die with them now? Perhaps the question is irrelevant he thinks. He is who and what he is; that is, he cannot help his disposition, despite the shame. When he had confessed the sin of cowardice to Fr Aloysius the day before, the priest listened seriously but did not judge him. To his surprise he laid both hands on his shoulders and his touch brought a kind of forgiveness. Some of his companions were a different sort and, if he is to be proud, it should be because at least he tried to be with them in this garden of their final work where everything planted could thrive on human blood only. To even grasp that mystery was, he supposes, his life's best work and perhaps he should feel proud after all.

He holds his breath. Footfalls now, not so sure-footed as one might imagine. He wonders perhaps if they are blind-folded, the three, including Plunkett, being led to the edge. He wishes to God he could see out, if he could, but the cell window and bars are impossibly high up. There is no means of raising himself. If he too could only stand there, in the yard, to follow them in a comradely way to their final moments.

The sound, when it comes, is familiar. Apart from the shouted orders, the heavy click of the rifles, the mathematical rhythm of their executioners' feet. Then another shout and then the point-blank volleys splitting the air, ripping the city to pieces. In the silence that follows he hears again the thrushes and blackbirds of Kilmainham in the early May morning, hears living creatures respond to what is instinctive as the year spins towards summer.

Then above the birdsong his ears catch the sound of the outraged and weeping who have gathered beyond the gaol. He picks his pencil up off the floor and rams it in his pocket, then falls to his knees in an effort at desperate prayer, as the souls of the blessed rise over the city.

MRS WARD'S DIARY
Dublin

Despite his best intentions Francis could not avert his eyes from the open pages of his mother's diary. She had left it in the morning room, having interrupted her daily writing to visit Dr Armstrong who had recently taken new rooms on Fitzwilliam Square. In the months since the April disturbances she had felt unwell. She suffered with rheumatic ache in both hips, the effect of this being that she felt impeded in her normal activities.

Francis had gone in to read the morning paper. He was eager to catch the political reports, to read them without having to break his concentration in order to listen to Mother's latest wisdom. He had chosen his moment and savoured the prospect of sitting in the green high-backed armchair, his back to the east-facing morning window where sunlight would stream comfortably over his shoulders and illuminate the oil-scented print of a fresh copy of *The Irish Times*.

His glance fell on the open diary as he passed his mother's bureau and there it lodged, as if attached by an invisible adhesive.

October 20th 1916, he read rapidly:

Today being Friday I have no regrets that the week is at a close. Neither of my children has ever been consistently wise but Francis, in particular, has given me more cause for concern than I feel is fair, between his politics and the risks he has taken – no, his admirable bravery in April, and indeed I like to think that dear Harold would have been proud of his courageous son, but now this latest episode – the alliance with that woman – is it friendship, I ask myself? Is it an infatuation? Pray God it is a passing fancy. We can do without any more foreign complications encroaching on the peace of the household, for it is bad enough that Margaret is in Burma. Thank God also for the patience of paper that can contain my honest thoughts since I have recourse to no ear in the eleven years since Harold's death and, although she always replies, letters to poor Margaret don't adequately satisfy my need for a sympathetic hearing. She has enough concerns of her own out in Mandalay and the health of baby Henry to consider as well as her own increasingly delicate condition in that torrid climate. William really ought not to have persuaded her to travel. But I digress. My concern today is about that woman and the unhealthy attachment Francis has forged with someone we know absolutely nothing about. I wonder who she is and what sort of people she comes from and furthermore whether Francis has considered the risks should he …

At this point, the narrative was interrupted. He stood very still as he read, the pupils of his blue eyes sharp as pinpricks as he scanned his mother's forward-slanted hand, unwilling to do more than look at this single page. If she were to see him now she would be horrified at his treachery but – if he was honest – he had never had any scruples about reading material which others left carelessly lying about. If a letter or an account lay open in the morning room at breakfast he would automatically glance at it. And some years before he had been an eager reader of his sister's diary, especially during her intense attachment to one of the Sisters at Muckross Park College. If a thing was so precious to the writer they would lock it away no matter what, he justified himself, and furthermore this propensity to acquire information from whatever source, had made him useful to his comrades in the Irish Citizen Army when the time to fight had come the previous Easter.

On the other hand he experienced the cold realisation that one reads at one's own peril what someone else assumes to be private and in this spirit felt piqued that Mother should refer to both he and Margaret as never having been 'consistently wise'. Mother herself was never consistently anything except believing herself to be correct in all her opinions and, philanthropic though her nature was, generous and progressive in some respects – after all, she had been proud of his political activities – she nonetheless retained at times a mysterious and peace-fracturing code of expectation where her family was concerned.

Annoyed, Francis abruptly turned on his heel, smacked the newspaper against his thigh before flinging it on the chaise longue and left the room. *That woman.* How dare she refer to the exotic visitor in such a manner.

That the remarkable woman was simply passing through Ireland on a brief and possibly ill-conceived tour he had already accepted. But for Mother to refer to her so lightly, to dismiss her as of no consequence as if she were some vagrant gypsy – was another matter entirely. He almost wished he had not read the blasted diary now but on the other hand it would give him some advantage when it came to handling Mother. He would now know how to behave, how *not* to speak of his new friend and generally to conduct himself with the evasive ease a young man of twenty-three might assume with a parent and when done with politics and his male companions.

He had met Anna one evening two months before when he tried to enter one of the city's older public houses. Distracted by a commotion in the doorway of the establishment he saw a tall dark-haired woman imperiously weave a red shawl around her shoulders, crossing it on her chest as she attempted to leave. The shawl caught his eye, stitched and appliqued as it was with delicate peacocks' tails in blue and green. Two men were delaying her. She looked flushed and embarrassed if not also slightly afraid. One of them was in the process of blocking her passage through the doorway just as Francis approached.

'Let me go, plez!'

At this, her would-be captor copycatted her accent and replied that he could not let such a pretty woman go. She tried to push past him but his companion intervened to catch her by the arm and drew her back. Unbalanced she swung the small purse which dangled from her wrist at him, missed, and the purse then fell heavily to the ground. Francis frowned as the contents within broke and immediately a dark puddle spread beneath the sequinned purse's silky fabric.

'Oh, oh!' the woman was almost weeping at this stage. She knelt down and grappled for her purse which dripped liquid as she pulled away from the men. The sweet pungency of spilt whiskey rose on the air and reached Francis's nostrils. One of them lunged at her, an unshaven fellow with two pegs for front teeth and a large belly.

Instinct made Francis intervene. 'Leave the lady alone!' he urged, glaring at the men.

The unshaven one cursed before turning to his friend and grumbling something incoherent.

'Foreigners,' the friend, who was more sober, called out. 'Ireland needs her own!'

Francis held his nerve. Two burly fellows like this held no threat but even so he distrusted them. There had been bloody incidents in recent weeks within the public houses, rows had started and a firearm was drawn in The Golden Harp in Townsend Street. He did not wish to see blood spilt or life lost. Not that there was any serious risk of that occurring here he realised. After all the tall lady was now standing by his side, her inquisitive face turned towards his.

'I leave hotel to buy bottle of good spirit to heat body!' she explained breathlessly, 'This country is so *cooold*, hotel not warm, not good for bones and voice. I am a singer.'

Surprised at this rush of information Francis gathered himself. Accustomed as he was to certain women it was clear even to one as experienced as he regarded himself to be that the lady before him belonged to a different category of femaleness, at least not one he had previously encountered.

Almost but not quite as tall as he, she turned a heart-shaped face with a firm but not too pointed chin towards him and smiled brilliantly. Her eyes were the colour of Mother's aquamarine pendant and her abundant raven-black hair was loosely plaited in an attractive mound that sagged in half-collapse towards the nape of her elegant neck. Her skin was pale but this was no freckled pallor and her eyes seemed all the more brilliant and wild against such a smooth, ivory complexion. She was, he thought, feeling inspired, like something someone had painted, a subject for one of those new artists in Montparnasse whose work he had chanced to see on a visit to Paris two years before. He was thinking of Soutine and Modigliani and what they might have done with this face.

He forced himself eventually to speak. 'I – I can accompany you in safety to your hotel, Miss –'

'Basheva.'

'I beg your pardon?'

'Anna Basheva. Thank you,' she said grandly, relaxing the most delicate of wrists as she proffered the back of her right hand. Flustered, he grasped and shook it. The smallest of knowing smiles flickered across her face.

They turned onto Grafton Street before she pointed towards St Stephen's Green.

'Hotel is here,' she announced.

As they walked she held the still-dripping purse at a remove from her clothing. The hem of a blue dress fell below a black velvet coat and the red shawl was now thrown carelessly around her shoulders. She could have been a wandering gypsy, he thought, with the gold hoop earrings, her ornate floral brooch and many bangles. At the same time he knew that she was no such thing, that the aristocratic bearing, the straight shoulders and gently swaying hips indicated someone very sure of their position on the earth.

He left her at the hotel entrance. It was one of the cheaper ones, though perfectly respectable for all that. They stood for some minutes and talked within a wan gaslight beneath the small canopy outside. She did not invite him within, nor did he suggest it, but the conversation uncoiled easily. Once she established a few facts about him – especially his occupation, which seemed to concern her – he found her to be an avid conversationalist when the subject was herself and her activities.

'We must talk. Again tomorrow, yes?' she enquired, tilting her head coquettishly.

For a moment he was lost for words. Could he meet her the next day? Of course he could. The law course he had interrupted earlier that year but which he had recently resumed was not so demanding that he could not afford to miss some lectures. They said goodnight and he caught a tram on Harcourt Street, then drifted homewards in a reverie.

When he got in Mother was in a flap in the dining room. He had missed dinner, he had missed a visit from Aunt Hilda, there was a leak in the scullery and they would have to get someone to fix it. Moreover his sister Margaret's latest missive from Mandalay informed them that poor William had caught malaria and was most unwell, although not in any immediate danger.

'At least the child is spared!' Mother exclaimed, shaking her head in annoyance.

'Yes,' Francis conceded. 'It would not go well if the little fellow caught it.'

At the very idea of little Henry catching malaria Mother began to excite herself again and worked herself into such a lather that Francis took a hard look at her. Mother was increasingly hysterical, he thought, and wondered why this might be.

'What did Dr Armstrong say?' he asked as casually as possible in an effort to glean information regarding her health and also to change the subject.

'Dr Armstrong?' For a moment she seemed again unsettled. 'Oh, he says I must use hot and cold compresses and if possible visit a spa and take seaweed baths. I said to him, I said "Dr Armstrong, how in heaven's name do you think I can manage a spa when my days are committed between hospital visits, between the question of the vote and our rights as women?" I looked at him quite directly as I said this but he only smiled and replied that our rights as women would be as intact after a visit to a spa as they were before it. In other words, Francis, he doesn't take the question of votes for women seriously. I could see that, but I said nothing. I held my peace.'

She shook her head and gave an amused little laugh.

'So, Mother, will you visit a spa then?'

'I have considered it. I may go to Kilkee. Perhaps in two weeks if I can arrange it. There is a Ladies' Committee meeting regarding improving conditions in the lying-in hospital and also talk of a visit to London to the Women's Social and Political Union – I cannot be absent from that at this critical point.'

Francis said nothing. He welcomed Mother's absences. It would be a relief to have the house to himself. He could invite around his companions, including the ones she did not approve of, and they could smoke and drink into the small hours without fear of disturbing anybody. Sometimes they included a few young women in the company, but only the gayest and the best dancers, and the hall and dining room would resound with laughter and lively discussion.

Sometimes he thought Mother was not as well as she used to be. Was it her time of life, he wondered vaguely, without wanting to dwell on that too much or was something more sinister working in her body? Dr Armstrong never provided great insight into her condition but it was clear to Francis that she had developed a new and sometimes alarming nervousness. In any event she was going away and fairly soon. He took out a cigarette, tapped it gently and relaxed at the thought of her absence.

'And you, dear? What have you done today since lectures finished?'

Despite his intention to say nothing he described the encounter with the woman and his rescuing her from two disreputable characters. Mother regarded him steadily as he spoke.

'Be careful, Francis. That's all I'll say. Just be careful.'

'Oh, Mother!'

'She is – not from the Continent, I take it?'

'She is from Russia.'

'A White Russian!' There was a perceptible pause. 'How interesting.'

'I don't know that. I didn't ask. In any case, I'm to meet with her tomorrow.'

He lit his cigarette and took a deep pull, his eyes closing slightly.

Mother drew herself up. 'I've said my piece and now I'm going to bed,' she announced, turning and leaving the dining room. He listened to the sound of her heels as she crossed the hallway and took the stairs.

As it turned out Mother did not visit the spa in Kilkee but remained in the city and attended many meetings with other women and the scattering of suffragette-supporting husbands who shared their wives' aims. She had limited time to be at home which suited Francis perfectly in the weeks that followed.

As planned, he met Anna Basheva the next afternoon outside her hotel. From the outset she complained loudly about the hotel room and its inadequacy. It was small and too cold and very *very* bad for her voice. She would really *love* to be able to move to a better class of accommodation. They walked to Nassau Street and entered the Polidor Tearooms. He watched as she scanned the menu, her eyes moving carefully down the card before she decided on black tea and an eclair.

Everything about her hinted that Mother was right about being careful but he was not one whose life had been guided by shrewdness, besides which he had never before encountered a woman so exciting and also beautiful. What else could he do but spend time with her?

Clearly she considered him to be wealthy, a view of which he attempted to disabuse her. But it was all relative. Where she had come from, she announced sorrowfully, social conditions had declined to such an extent that most of the people in her town were impoverished.

'We have nothing! In Chisinău thirteen years ago, the crowds cry "Kill the Jews! Kill the Jews!"'

In her halting English she explained how families were gradually deprived of their businesses and how the rumour spread that Jews who wrote up their accounts in Yiddish were swindling the ordinary Russian customer. She went on to describe how the people were slaughtered like animals and that she saw one baby – a little baby barely three months old – torn to pieces in the frenzy. At this memory her eyes did not fill up with tears but glazed over as if she could see the whole atrocity right there before her as she spoke. Her shoulders slumped.

The tea and eclairs arrived. To his surprise her appetite had vanished and she seemed unable to eat. She picked dispiritedly at the sweet pastry for a few moments then sipped her tea before pushing both away.

'We … we have had our troubles here,' Francis stammered, feeling inexperienced and too young.

'Not like our troubles.' She cut the air with her hand and shook her head. 'We hear about your troubles. I read newspaper in Paris in summer. I know what Lenin say too about Ireland. Sympathetic. But your troubles, not the same. You not a stranger in strange land like Russian Jews! You no see baby murders.'

She was right. At least he felt he was an Irishman and that even under the British his Irishness was complete in every way except that he could not vote for an Irish parliament. He could read what he wished, could see all the new films, could pray in whichever church he chose and could also speak freely and trade with whom he wished. But his form of Irishness, he knew, also had to do with his class. He might feel differently if he lived in one of the tenements. There he would witness parallels between Anna's Jews – who had no social or economic freedoms – and some of his own countrymen.

But he did not say this. Instead he took her hand and held it in his. Her fingernails were elegantly filed with a pale sheen of pink lacquer so that they struck him as little shells.

'How long will you stay in Dublin?' he asked.

'Until I have money for ship to America.'

'You have not booked the passage?'

'Not until I save enough money.'

'I will help you if I can. A little.'

At this she turned her head towards him and smiled helplessly, adorably.

'You would do this – for me?'

'It's what friends do, isn't it?' he replied, feeling a little foolish. He was not completely blind to the direction in which he was headed.

'Faithful friends,' she agreed.

'I can't give you all the money. Only some,' he cautioned, foreseeing a substantial withdrawal from his bank account and the rapidly dwindling inheritance which Mother had passed to him and Margaret in separate amounts after Father's death.

'But you give. You give with heart and not count cost.'

She leant over and, pressing her lips against his cheek, held them there lightly for a moment before withdrawing again.

Her mood had brightened. As well as several other concerts throughout Ireland – including one in Enniskillen and another in Cork – she would be singing in the Antient Concert Rooms the following Friday night and had heard that it was the only prominent place for a visiting performer. Was this true? Would he attend?

Francis's grasp of music was largely limited to the local piping from the city's public houses, Christmas carols in the University Church and threads of choir songs from his days attending Belvedere but he had heard Count John McCormack in full voice only four years before, while Mother had once commandeered Margaret to a recital by the strange and controversial new writer Mr Joyce. But that was many years before, and Margaret – even if she were there – might not even remember the occasion. Mr Joyce, though, was an accomplished singer and it was beyond Francis as to why he had turned his back on his own lyrical tenor voice. The world was full of scribblers scratching their gloom-ridden lines but there was a dearth of the brightness of music, he thought.

'Of course I will attend,' he replied after a pause.

'I will sing one Irish song. Repertoire is mostly Russian – some Yiddish melody too – but one Irish song. For you.'

As he blushed and tried not to look too pleased he dared not ask what the song might be.

Dressed to go out three days later he wondered if the concert would be well attended. One never knew, even if the Antient Concert Rooms was a popular venue for many kinds of entertainment. Once he had watched a feeble magician fumbling with pigeons and hats and having no workable tricks at all. The one trick he had accomplished was to find coins behind people's ears. Even so many had deserted the theatre before the performance concluded.

Before he left that evening he listened carefully, his ears sharpening to pick up Mother's orientation in the house. But all was silent. He assumed she was resting. He slipped quietly into the sitting room and opened her bureau, which remained unlocked. The diary was there. Quickly he flipped it open to the day's date. Nothing. He turned back a page. She had written very little recently.

> Dr Armstrong's new rooms are very grand and stylish. No surprises there. A new John Lavery on the wall of his reception room also. I must tell Margaret that she will have to travel to Fitzwilliam Square if she wishes to see him on her return to Ireland. She will need a thorough examination after all she has been through. He suggested another appointment as he is not completely happy with my progress. Thank heavens for his prudence.

He slammed it shut quickly, pushed it back to its original position and closed the lid of the bureau. It was time to leave, time to hear Anna. As he pulled the porch door shut and walked down the path to the street he felt slightly sick with excitement and anticipation. He had intended to hail a cab but changed his mind and decided to walk to the theatre. The walk would calm him.

On Brunswick Street it seemed as if all Dublin had turned out in force. He paused before the yellow poster with its red and black announcement:

To-night at 8 p.m. Matinee, tomorrow Saturday, at 2 p.m. Madame Anna Basheva, World-Renowned Russian Mezzo-Soprano Performing in Antient Concert Rooms, Gigantic Success for Finale of GRAND EUROPEAN TOUR, including Madrid, Budapest, Vienna, Rome, Berlin, Paris and now DUBLIN!

Inside he spotted some of Mother's cronies on the other side of the foyer but beyond nodding by way of greeting he did not delay and went straight to his seat. No doubt she would soon know about his outing. His seat was not as far forward as he would have liked but he felt certain that when Anna took a final bow her lovely eyes would pick him out from the general rabble.

Francis checked his watch at four minutes past the hour, the conductor tapped the music stand and the quartet of two violins, one viola and a cello struck up a brief Russian-sounding melody, set in a minor key. A dance song perhaps, but not an entirely happy one, he thought. Then, when the audience had applauded and settled themselves, out stepped Anna Basheva, dressed head to toe in a black lacy gown with sea-green velvet piping on its ruffled sleeves. Her hair was twisted up high on her head and fixed in place with an ivory comb and a few sparkling hairpins. She held herself very straight as she neared the front of the stage, then bowed graciously to her audience. Even from where he sat he could see the eagerness and delight in her face, the desire of the performer to perform, to be the best she could possibly be.

The programme would commence with three Russian dance-melodies from east of the Volga, she explained, before entering a song cycle inspired by the tragedy of the Jews and their long journey through history. At this point, she paused and sighed as if it was all too much to bear. She gave a little shrug then proceeded again.

'But! I do not forget the great classical composers,' she explained. 'And later I sing from Tchaikovsky, Rimsky-Korsakov, Schubert and finally I will sing an Irish song!'

At this the audience burst into applause and she bowed again before drawing herself up, chest forward and shoulders straight. Her arms hung free, neither limp nor stiff, finding the necessary level of tension between ease and strain which suited the mechanism of her voice.

Francis's attention did not flag. Occasionally he stole a look around the theatre to see how she was being received. Some of the usual grandees he recognised – those who would automatically receive invitations from theatre establishments but who never paid for their seats, the honorary, tightly-knit population of the city to whom culture belonged and whose voices and opinions on this or that singer, writer or artist were known to all, and sometimes influential. It was difficult to read from their carefully-set expressions exactly what they thought. But the rest of the audience, the real people, were charmed. Women leaned forward, their eyes avid as they feasted on the singer, for it was not alone her voice that bewitched. She was a complete work in which radiance was inseparable from a voice that, although good, he suspected was not what the critics might call 'world class'. It did not matter. The evening – and the people of Dublin – belonged in that moment to her.

When she finally opened her throat and the first notes of Mr Yeats's poem 'Down by the Salley Gardens' emerged, a ripple of spontaneous applause circled the theatre. Despite himself Francis's eyes grew moist, his throat tightened. That folk song, that simplest of airs, had the capacity to drag him deep into his own heart to the desert that lay there, unwatered by love. Even Anna, whom he had met so recently, would soon go, evaporating like dew on the morning grass. What time had he had, he ruminated as she sang for his own heart, when he had given so much of it to political causes and after that to entertainment? Perhaps it was time to make room for more than the destiny of a nation. He was fortunate to still have a life to live, unlike some of his companions.

As Anna's voice descended slowly towards the final notes of the song – he could hear it, that lamenting high *doh*, falling to *soh, lah, soh, me, ray, doh-doh* ... and how the voice held, tremulous yet strong in the face of lost love. She stood a moment, eyes downcast, hands joined modestly as the orchestra slowed through the final cadence.

The response was rapturous. His cheeks flamed with pleasure as curtain call followed curtain call and an encore was called for. By now some of the gentlemen were stamping their feet as they called out *Bravo! Bravo!* For some moments it seemed as if she was not going to reappear until suddenly she tripped gaily onto the stage again. The audience quietened down and soon there was total silence.

'This time, ladies and gentlemen of Dublin,' she began in an intimate, joking voice to which they applauded before she could go further, 'I bring you to *my* country again, to the river Volga, where the great, long boats sail down from the North all the way to the Caspian Sea. It is a beautiful river and here is my song of that river.'

It struck Francis that Anna's English had improved remarkably since she had taken to the stage but perhaps she had her introductions learned by heart. There were certainly none of the purring hesitations and grammatical errors he normally associated with her speech, even in their most intimate moments together.

Afterwards he went to her dressing room and embraced her. She flung her arms around his neck as if she had known him all her life.

'It was good, no? They like me, yes?'

'They loved you, Anna!' he cried, whirling her delightedly off her feet.

'Look, look! Kind people send flowers!'

It was true and he noted jealously that the room had *three* bouquets of blooms, as well as the basket of pink and yellow roses he had sent. The roses were dewy and fresh. She had not yet read his note.

'It appears you have other admirers,' he said softly, 'And no wonder, you are a genius!'

It was a view with which she seemed to concur.

When he was with her later that night he woke once and, finding her also awake, remarked what a pity it was that she had to depart for America. *Pity, pity,* she whispered in the dark, *but please not to think of such things, not now, my young love, not now ...*

The following morning she told him that she would leave in two weeks precisely.

'You did not come home last night, Francis,' his mother announced as he made to slip up the staircase at noon the next day.

'I did not, Mother,' he replied in the calmest voice he could muster.

It took him all of his power to control his emotions and conceal the fact that his world – no, his life – had changed.

His mother scrutinised him carefully but said nothing. She was again hurrying out, this time to arrange Father's anniversary Mass, and arranged her hat before the long hallway mirror. She would attend many Masses because she liked to begin her remembrance Masses a week or so in advance of the actual date. She did not exert the slightest pressure on Francis to attend these, merely remarking that the nature of the relationship between a husband and a wife was a secret and wonderful matter for each and that she greatly missed it. He watched as she left, flooded with relief at her distractedness. He would be alone again, even if for a few hours.

Having twice read Mother's diary a seed of great curiosity had taken root in Francis's heart. He knew that he would transgress again but that also it was something he might pass on to Fr Aloysius some Saturday morning in the confessional. That was the great thing about Confession. Afterwards came the most wonderful feeling of cleanliness, as if all that had been wrong, thoughtless or downright immoral had been quickly dissolved in the spirit of forgiveness and repentance. How often he intended to repent and how often he failed! But that was understood by him and his like to be the nature of their faith. There was always another Confession which he could attend and another one after that and he was no less serious in his intentions even if he sinned again.

Once more he read his mother's private words feeling as ashamed even as he felt it a duty to himself.

The room was silent. At a quarter past twelve in the afternoon nobody had thought to lift the cover off the canary's cage. The canary was a recent acquisition of Mother's and the cage was large and roomy enough although Francis did not, in principle, approve of birds in cages. He lifted the cloth and peered in at the creature. It stirred and began to sing. Despite himself he smiled and poked one finger through the gilded grid but the bird was not inclined to move from its perch. He wiggled his finger again. This time it edged cautiously along the perch, sideways but in his direction. It was very close now, the feathers slightly ruffled, making Francis wonder if the room was actually warm enough. He lifted the cage and brought it to the window, laying it on a small octagonal table. The sun streamed in, although white clouds raced across the sky, but it was warmer and to Francis's eye it seemed that the bird's feathers flattened. Again it sang, but intermittently.

He turned his attention to his mother's open bureau. The diary was there as usual but closed. However the leather flap that wound around and clicked into a small buckle at the front was not locked. He pressed it and it sprang open.

At Mass over the past days I have prayed for clarity in a number of matters. It is possible that I am as foolish as Francis appears to be. He is making a fool of himself with the Russian and even his appearance has begun to suffer. For one who has always been the essence of the dapper young gent about town he has fallen to a state of what I can only describe as ennui and loucheness. I sincerely hope he remains in good health and that nothing unsavoury – oh, but I cannot think of such things. Pray that he has some good sense left in that love-enfeebled brain of his! He scarcely bothers to shave. He smokes even more than ever and insists now on buying black Russian cigarettes from Foxes. I am hoping the woman finally departs on her ship to America! She is too old for Francis, even if everything else were in order and he knows nothing about her. Dear Dr A advises me to say little but to sit it out. He is most likely very wise but as a mother I find it difficult to hold my peace if I believe something to be amiss with either of my children.

Regarding Dr A, no improvement in my rheumatics but then I have still not taken his advice about spa treatments. He did, however, highly recommend the use of a new and apparently stimulating medical invention which men and women with various health conditions find brings very pleasant relief. The device is called the Violet Wand and is regarded as being at the forefront of appropriate pain relief for adults. He has written a prescription and I shall send to London for one forthwith. The fact is I do not wish to travel all the way to Kilkee to be wrapped in seaweed without a companion. I am an independent woman in my way but at this point in my life I long for companionship. I have confided as much to Dr A. He reassures me that my needs are not in the least unusual, indeed that if he were free – this he has conveyed in a most subtle manner – he would come calling if I were to permit it. Such an admission! I can't say I am not flattered. Well that is all in the realm of the impossible and my sense of virtue permits no such indelicacies, which brings me back to the question of Francis. His dear father would spin in his grave if he knew of his son's debauched life. And after all he had achieved as a young man earlier this year! I am beside myself with worry. Well, that's enough for today. I await the post and more news from Margaret. William is recovering well by her account and little Henry is strong and perhaps, after all, God still remains in His heaven.

So his manner was 'debauched', was it? Feeling grim yet slightly amused Francis replaced the diary and left the room. Now Mother was giving *him* cause for concern with her fanciful suggestions regarding Dr Armstrong and his odd-sounding prescription. Dr Armstrong! The idea of it. The man who had been their family doctor for years was a gentleman not given – to Francis's knowledge – to flagrant behaviour. Yet the diary entry suggested otherwise. Or did it? In fact, Dr Armstrong seemed to speak quite honourably, if Mother's account was reliable. He spoke in the conditional future. What *would* or *might* happen *if* he were free, which of course he was not. Mrs Armstrong was one of the guiding lights of the city's children's choir, and much alive despite what Dr Armstrong might fancy.

There and then as he climbed the stairs to his bedroom he decided he would not read Mother's diary ever again. Apart from the deception of it, the risk of information was more than he could bear. She wrote openly and flowingly and what she did not say directly she implied and that was more than enough to unsettle him.

But it was too late. Two days later as he was forking up the last morsels of his breakfast kippers and toast Mother stormed into the room, face flaming.

'You have been reading my private writings!' she thundered, placing the diary onto the table beside him.

Aghast he turned and looked at her, scarcely managing to swallow the last bite in his mouth.

'Despicable, despicable son! You forgot to close the lock when you had finished your rampage through my private thoughts!'

Now she clasped the diary she had just put down and struck him smartly on the side of the head, then on the shoulders, so that he shrank back and attempted to protect himself with crossed arms from the onslaught.

'I – I didn't mean to –' he stammered.

'To think I raised a son who is so untrustworthy that he would actually raid his own Mother's private observations. I blame myself entirely for ill-rearing and not providing you with a code of moral conduct to guide your behaviour.'

'Mother, please don't blame yourself,' Francis pleaded, stumbling to his feet, his chair falling back on the floor. 'I'm entirely to blame. I'm a scurrilous cad to have done such a thing and I will never forgive myself. It's just that the first time it really was a question of being tempted – your pages lay wide open one morning – and I accidentally read them.'

'There is no accident in this, Francis, any more than there is any accident in the way that woman has ensnared you and is determined to hold onto you until she has got what she wants. Remember, Francis, if you empty your accounts in the bank for her I am not in a position to replenish the loss.'

They lapsed into silence for some moments. He began to pace the room up and down along the dining table, rattled by the unpredictable change in direction which her accusations had taken. She stood where she was, looking puzzled and angry.

'This has hurt me deeply,' she eventually said.

'What are you referring to? The diary or Anna?'

'Anna! You speak of her as if she was a bosom companion.'

'And you, Mother, about something which is none of your business.'

'Nor was the reading of my diary your business.'

He did not speak. The sound of a tram rumbling in the distance broke the momentary silence. The canary gave a slow, high whistle and hopped from one side of the cage to the other.

'You hurt me deeply,' she took up.

'I know. I am sorry.'

'And despite what you may be thinking about –'

'Dr Armstrong?'

'Oh for heaven's sake, is nothing of mine to be private?'

'Mother, nothing of mine was so private either that you did not feel free to judge me and assume the worst about Anna Basheva – and me.'

She fidgeted with the buttons on the front of her dress.

'As your Mother – I naturally fear that the wrong kind of woman might –'

'What? Take me away? Or simply love me?'

To this she had no reply.

'She loves me.'

'Don't be ridiculous, Francis. That woman has lived on her wits, conniving her way across Europe from city to city. Madrid! Budapest! Vienna! Do you really believe she has *sung* in all these places or in any place that counts with the cultural classes?' His mother scoffed outright and threw her eyes to the ceiling. 'She is without a manager. She arrives in a city and works her way into the right company for a certain period, wining and dining with them from what I hear, then manages to fool a quartet of musicians to accompany her in the Antient Concert Rooms. She's an expert – can't you see that, son? She finds whatever fools will put up with her and her nonsense, before moving on again.'

He was stung by this, by its possibilities. It could not be true. He was the one, the special one.

'She loves me,' he repeated softly, although trembling.

His Mother did not respond. She snatched up the diary again. A vein down the centre of her forehead pulsed as she contained her agitation.

'At best, you are perhaps her muse. Her sort always like to have a muse or two to *inspire* them. God help your innocence!'

Francis gasped. It was true. Anna had once, in the throes of passion, called him her muse. He had been flattered. For a moment, though, he said nothing because in his Mother's mouth the word suddenly seemed tawdry, less than what it could be.

'In any event,' she went on, 'I pray you'll come to your senses.'

Now he was stung. 'Blast my senses and blast your praying! What about your own, seeing as sense concerns you? I believe you too are not devoid of romantic feeling if I have understood correctly!'

She struck him with her hand hard across the face.

'How *dare* you!'

The force of it made him stagger and he rubbed his jaw, mouth hanging open with the shock of it as she turned to leave the room. Already he could taste blood in his mouth where the tender flesh within his cheeks had broken against his teeth.

Francis and Mother did not speak for almost two weeks. They avoided one another conspicuously, he rising earlier than usual so as not to run into her at breakfast. As much as possible he dined out on St Stephen's Green, often with Anna. She had secured three more bookings around the city as well as an engagement with the gentry of Aylesmere Castle in County Kildare. But the time for her departure was approaching and it was a matter of savouring hours and moments when he could be with her. Although she always seemed happy – no, overjoyed – to see him, he could not help but feel that he did not know her. On the other hand she certainly knew him because he had not held back anything about himself. She knew about his allegiance to the Irish Citizen Army and of his passion for Ireland's freedom. She knew too that he had never loved a woman before, that she was his first fleshly passion, something that had made her eyes even more brilliant, her kisses that bit more ardent. She said everything he wished to hear, proved herself a good and vivacious conversationalist, well-versed in all the great cultural movements. If anything she informed *him* about the movements of all the most important singers and composers of the day – after all she had met most of them and could tell him exactly what Diaghilev had said to Nijinsky after the controversial opening performance of *Le Sacré du Printemps* at the Théâtre des Champs-Élysées three years before. She herself had been there and witnessed the whole riotous s*candale*, and it was Nijinsky's dancing – not Stravinsky's music – which prompted the storm.

Francis took her word for it. How could he respond? He had never seen a ballet, never mind a modern one. The only cultural riot he had heard about was when *The Playboy of the Western World* had dismayed the delicate sensibilities of the Dublin audience on its opening night nine years before. She rambled on as they strolled through St Stephen's Green, around flaming autumnal beds of begonias, near the pond, her arm slipped easily through his. She listed the names of those who knew her and who had proven themselves to be exceptional allies during her travels. There was Schoenberg, of course, and Caruso – 'Oh, dear Enrico, so kind to me when I come to Italy!' – and the *magnificent* Russian bass Feodor Chaliapin. ('You do not know Chaliapin? How strange! Well, no matter, take it from me that he is exceptional man, exceptional!'). As she talked on, Francis's eye drifted to the tops of the trees, golden in the late afternoon, and beyond that to the dusky roofs of the high-bricked buildings beyond the Green. A few leaves drifted down brushing his shoulders. How vast the world was, he thought, and how well Anna knew it. If she knew all these people, he pondered, why should she even think of America? What was in America for her?

She had no family there but claimed to have a new manager waiting for her in New York who would meet her the very moment she disembarked from the ship. Together they would develop her career.

'But it will be – surely it will be very difficult? A woman, alone?'

She turned to him and pulled gently at his hand. 'I look like woman who not survive? Main problem is money. *Very* difficult career, always, always. Other problem is I am Jew. But in America that not matter so much. No pogrom. No killing childs before my eyes.'

In the moments of silence that followed, during which she grew absent and despondent just as she had been in the Polidor Tearooms, something slipped into place and he recognised what had been missing, a version of something closer to truth. He saw the village perhaps in winter, food shortages, a maddened mob, the confusion and upheaval of new rules and no rules, the blurring of boundaries of behaviour as the tribe began its purge. The ousting of the obvious ones.

'Was it – was that *your* child, Anna? Did those people kill your *baby*? Your –' He could scarcely get the words out. 'Your *little one*?'

At this she merely shuddered. He caught her hand.

'Tell me!'

She nodded and lowered her face, chewing her bottom lip. She gave a harsh sigh and blinked a few times, struggling for control.

'Is new country and someday I no longer stranger in a strange country. Understand?'

Now so much was clear to him. The elusiveness, the bewitching gaiety, the need to impress, the need to secure her life and begin again.

He had never felt himself a stranger in a strange country until relatively recently. Everything had changed when the heroic Volunteers were executed in May. Before that he had deluded himself that his country was as familiar – and welcoming – to him as any he could imagine. It was not entirely the case, as he and the others who fought and eventually the people of Ireland came to see. In their own country, which was not yet a nation, they were being treated as strangers. In Anna's case it was worse. Starving hounds had always pursued the hare that danced the open field.

Even so he struggled right up to the morning of her departure from Kingsbridge Station to make his feelings for her grow slightly cooler. She was bound for Cork and then on to Queenstown where she would board the *Atlantica* and sail out of his life forever. They took a jaunting cart to the station. When they dismounted he insisted on carrying some of her baggage. A porter took the weighty trunk, leaving Francis with several hat-boxes, and one small needle-stitch valise, quite worn and threadbare. Within the station people moved busily. The Cork train was waiting and passengers hurried along the platform in twos and threes. How alone she was, he thought, with her baggage of losses so invisibly buried within the colourful self she presented to the world. And yet as he looked at her now she was not sad. The aquamarine eyes were bright and eager. She would not miss him very deeply, despite her endearments, despite the sweet kisses and how she had pressed him to her bosom for many nights, clinging to him in the little rooftop hotel room. She had already missed a child – painfully, deeply. There could only be a small corner in her heart for him.

He did not need to know more, if more there was. What did it matter if we do not uncover every single detail of another's past? Mother had tried to poison him against her. She had not succeeded in that but she had nonetheless planted too much doubt. At least, he consoled himself, he had continued to behave as if he had no doubts. And now, Anna Basheva was leaving. They walked down the platform towards First Class, the one thing he had insisted on. One last embrace, one last deep kiss, regardless of who was observing, a gentle stroke of her hand to his cheek, a playful brush of his eyebrows with her slim fingers and yet another kiss – and she turned away and stepped into the carriage. He watched, one hand in his pocket, the other adjusting his hat, as she settled herself within. His heart pounded. She should be looking out at him. Why was she not looking out? Impatience danced through his veins, God in heaven, she should be looking out into his eyes through that window! But then she was. Having sat down and arranged herself and the valise, having adjusted her hat to the correct playful tilt, she turned and smiled at him. He came closer to the window. She pushed her face closer, her plump pink lips forming words he could not hear. The train had begun to pull away, slowly. Plumes of steam rose around him, he heard the clunking engagement of pistons, iron. He quickened his pace. What was she saying? He peered in, mouthing *what?* back at her. Still he could not grasp her words. She repeated them. He heard nothing. Then again and she appeared to be shouting. Now he was joyous, although he still had not heard her and she could have been saying anything. But he could see her eyes and that was enough. Surely she loved him! He ran like a boy as the train picked up speed, legs stretching as he pounded the platform, roaring after her, *I love you, dearest Anna, please don't go!*

Unembarrassed, having transcended all ordinary shames and constraints by now, tears streamed from his eyes until eventually he could not keep up and the train pulled and ground its way faster and faster out of

Kingsbridge, taking the first long curve towards Inchicore as it headed south.

The next morning, for the first time in two weeks, Francis joined his Mother at breakfast. She asked no questions at first, but noted that he had shaved. His face was deathly pale after a sleepless night and she sensed new distress as she observed him.

'You will dine in this evening, Francis?' she quietly asked, opening the post with a dagger-like blade.

'I think so,' he replied, picking at a slice of bacon, then cutting slowly into a sausage.

'I shall order some best fillet.'

He did not answer.

'Red meat keeps the blood strong,' she said again, watching him.

He nodded. His eye came to rest on an oblong package farther down the table. 'Mother, what's –?'

He stopped himself abruptly. His Mother glanced up.

'Dr Armstrong's recommendation,' she remarked quietly.

'Oh.'

'I shall be calling to Fitzwilliam Square later on.'

He looked again towards her, her brown hair rolled softly behind her ears, a lavender silk dress emphasising her still-slim form. Her complexion was healthy and smooth for a woman of her years and he had not heard her speak of rheumatic pain in some time. Even so it was of no interest to him where she was going that day and whether or not she was now communicating a message of some kind. Her writings and thoughts were her own and would be. What use was so much revelation, mother to son and son to mother? Surely the least they could do was leave one another alone in pursuit of what each one dreamed?

TUTTY'S MOTHER

For most of the term Gerard Hubbard had been unhappy. He had had news of a kind that was a contented priest's greatest dread. The Provincial had visited the school in the first week of December, bringing news of the Province in general, gathering information and conferring with the men. He did this every year and, at the age of sixty-four, Fr Hubbard was not expecting the news he received.

It happened in the usual way, yet made his day unusual. The scattering of priests from within the Order who resided in Clongowes Castle were called individually to convene with the Provincial. It was a matter of personal discussion, much of it pleasant. Bonds were renewed, old stories remembered in a sociable way, with the added understanding that either party could air any matters of concern that had not been addressed in the normal course of vocational life. In brief, the Provincial's arrival signalled a duty of care both to the priests and to the Order itself. Fr Hubbard was experienced in relation to the question of personal feelings towards his religious companions, confident of his own ability to translate instinctive like or dislike into something manageable, rational and, if necessary, anodyne. So it was with Mark Fitzmaurice, whom he had never actually liked, regarding him as an over-ambitious Provincial of enormous cunning and charm – a fatal combination in his view. But to date they had never clashed. He rarely thought of the Provincial beyond responding conversationally to titbits of library gossip as the older members of the Order let their tongues relax in the evening, as they wondered where in Europe, or even in America, the Provincial might be.

Fitzmaurice, it was widely known, was fond of travel. It was said that he loved his job because of the opportunity to visit new places and because it brought occasional access to the Vatican and those close to the heart of the empire, which he and his like would defend to the final breath. Despite his own reservations about Fitzmaurice, Fr Hubbard found this to be a diminishing assessment of the man who, single-handedly, had kept the Order in a state of some vitality despite the hum of shameful suggestions regarding excessive wealth and other matters that were more opaque, and sometimes passed person to person. Within the local community the priests held their heads high, as well they might, thought Fr Hubbard. There was dignity and a calm sense that no serious taint had so far besmirched Clongowes Wood College. Furthermore everybody knew that what was in the air were suggestions, but even suggestions are mere threads unless supported with a ballast of precise words, with nouns, verbs and a distinct narrative. There existing no such narrative in the common discourse, Fr Hubbard felt quietly confident that all was well.

Yet it was also remarked that so fond was Mark Fitzmaurice of migration for extended periods – his pretext being meetings and occasional retreats – that surely he had no opportunity to get to know the men whose fate he partly controlled.

This was certainly the view that Fr Hubbard carried away from his December mid-morning encounter when he could not help but close the library door a little more firmly than necessary as he left. Immediately he bumped into the recently-retired Captain Condron – who now oversaw the school archives and nabbed him in an urgent way, engaging him in conversation about a minor disagreement between himself and the school librarian. It was all hot air, Fr Hubbard decided, nevertheless playing his part pleasantly in the little script as if nothing untoward was in the air. Condron had been discharged from the Front two years before with a metal plate planted where part of his skull used to be. He was prone to episodic agitations.

By the time he shook the man off, Fr Hubbard was determined to get to his room in the Castle.

He needed to be alone. He climbed the stairs, pausing on the first floor before continuing to the second floor and managed to avoid meeting cleaning women or anybody else likely to be on the move at that time of day, shortly before lunch.

Thoughts of lunch made him feel queasy. He would forego it, would forego the table attendance in the priests' private refectory and the usual topics: more mumbling about newspaper headlines and the deaths on Armistice Day, unsurprising reactions throughout the city, in complete contrast to unbounded joy-making in London. There might be, as usual, some talk about a teaching staff member's fondness for spirits, indeed the whisper was that he had his own poteen still at home, while Fr Ford, who had an obsession with cleanliness and order, would probably wonder for the umpteenth time was anybody going to do anything about painting the cricket pavilion in good time for Parents' Day in the summer term.

He would have to pray. Praying might relieve him of his pain, his rage, his sense of the unfairness of it all. He entered private quarters, closing the door quietly and surveyed the room, which was painted a vigorous green and stretched out into one of the turret corners of the castle. Two years before the Rector had granted him permission to select the colour himself. It was what he thought of as a *man's* green. He loved his room. The sturdy black Spanish sixteenth-century crucifix his father had inherited and given him when he had entered as a young Scholastic forty-four years before hung above the bed head and on his carved oak *prie-dieu* an untidy stash of books – some Keats, Brooke and Tennyson, as well as pain-filled sonnets from one of their own men – Hopkins no less – awaited his attention.

Dear God, he called out to the Great Emptiness, *help me.*

After his years of service. After praying and working, bending his will to a state of inner calm which was compromised only by his interest in gravel-ball. After his attempts to mould the boys into teams of excellent sportsmen they were moving him elsewhere. Out of Clongowes. Into the city.

He turned his head quickly in response to a sound in the room to his left. That would be Fr Lenehan unrolling his measuring tape to check if his wall hangings and pictures had been disturbed by the Castle maids that morning. He would probably have a spirit level at the ready too, Fr Hubbard surmised. Fr Lenehan liked his pictures to be absolutely straight and equidistant and operated an innocuous regime of picture straightening throughout the school.

Fr Hubbard collapsed into an easy chair. Why couldn't the Provincial have selected Fr Lenehan for his little cull? Heaven knows, *he* spent enough time in the city, visiting the sick. If anything, he revelled in the mood of death in the tenements as much as in respectable homes. And in the hospitals as men gasped their last he was known to be just the man to stand at the foot of a bed, arms crossed, staring calmly at the dying patient as if daring the Devil to come near. Why not *him*?

From his right came what sounded like a liquid mush groaning through the pipes. The source was close to his own sink, he noted in exasperation, pushing the bathroom door. His private *toilette* was frequently interfered with by emanations from his other neighbour, to the right, Fr MacCarthy, who wasn't given to excessive washing but nonetheless had been responsible on several occasions for blockages which had necessitated a tradesman to come calling from the local village. Why couldn't the Provincial move *him*?

You're a most able man – he could still hear the Provincial's smooth tones as he gazed gently across the desk – *with much to give that is perhaps not being fully utilised in Clongowes ...* The murmuring and rationalising went on for some minutes, *and of course your contribution to the new sporting developments is greatly valued*, during which Fr Hubbard had not interrupted, such was his shock. The most devastating of things could be executed in the calmest of voices, *but the Order's vision can be realised in many forms, many environments*, as if it was as simple as turning on a tap – *there is a different kind of young man who could benefit from your care, Fr Hubbard* – or pouring a drink. No change at all in the entire universe. But they were wrong. An entire cosmos was about to be disabled because of this disastrous, ghastly mistake on the Provincial's part – or was it a mistake?

Perhaps it was some kind of stupid spite, going back to God knows what. After all hadn't he actually *taught* the man who was now his superior in the Order? He raked through his memory to uncover what sanction, what punishment, he had afflicted on Mark Fitzmaurice as a boy, carried forward to the present when he was at his most powerful. He had held a certain position in the school at that time and was often confided in by the then headmaster, Fr O'Connor. Absurd, he chided himself. The idea was nonsensical. Grown men didn't behave like that. But supposing he *did* recall some of the more brutal episodes of a time some twenty-three years before? Supposing he remembered 1893?

He squeezed at his memory. What would the Provincial remember? There had been unpleasantness, inevitably, that had gone uninterrupted for several terms. Nastiness. The headmaster had not intervened because he did not know, and even if he had he would probably have regarded it as a matter between boys. But one boy's mother had taken the train from County Westmeath to Dublin and from there to Sallins where she procured a Landau and a sleep-deadened man willing to drive her in the middle of the night as far as Clongowes. Once arrived, the driver waited outside, dimly lit by the carriage lanterns, Hubbard imagined, as she pounded on the double doors at the Castle entrance until the Fr Rector had come stumbling in his slippers and woollen dressing gown to open up. Fr Rector, shocked into silence for once, was unable to prevent the lady from scaling the stone stairway to the gallery and then making her way, as if she had an internal map of the school, to the boys' dormitory. Fr Hubbard, who, as part of his duties, slept in a small alcove at the end of the dormitory, was woken by the commotion. Once there, she shook her son Tomás Tutty to life and removed him, bag and baggage, still in his pyjamas. But not before catching hold of a slumbering, red-haired boy in the next bed, the ringleader, and ripping a tuft from his head.

Miraculously that was the end of it. Tutty never returned. The Provincial would remember some of that because he had been in the same class as Tutty, though he had not been affected by the episodes and nor was Fr Hubbard involved. He had always been a sound sleeper so whatever had transpired during the nights in the dormitory he was not aware of.

Or was he? He began to pace the room. As a young teacher he had felt intuitively that one in their care was being persecuted but assumed it would sort itself out according to natural order. In every group there were the strong and then the rest – the less strong. Weaklings.

That red-haired boy, who stumbled to dazed wakefulness to find strands of his own hair on the sheets beneath him, had been magnificent. Viking in appearance and performance, whether in cross-country runs, wielding the broadsword, or playing gravel ball. Fr Hubbard, hearing the racket and the mother's wounded voice as she led her son away, had not wanted to interfere for the sake of the school. Only for the sake of the school. But then there was Tutty, more than this boy's equal. There had rarely been a sportsman of his calibre, fine-boned as he was. In an ideal world the red-haired boy and he should have been natural companions on any team. But that was not to be. And Mrs Tutty's excoriating letter left the Order in no doubt about what had taken place. Her allegations, which as far as the school view went, remained allegations, concerned a series of incidents that had mounted, slowly and unrelentingly, led by a group of three who despised the young Westmeath boy for many things: his build, which was not bulky so much as contained, elegant strength, his academic and sporting competence and his speech defect. He possessed a lengthy, serpentine lisp that they aped and mocked. Furthermore the mother's account of the attitude of a young scholastic shook the Community to its roots. Some of the older priests blanched. Others resented the woman's nerve. Gerard Hubbard had observed the young priest-in-training who seemed bizarrely drawn to the boy and the goings-on around him, who was undoubtedly aware of deliberately planted insects in the boy's bed, of middle-of-the-night latrine-bowl treatment, the salting of his dessert and the sugaring of his dinner. He had, apparently, tried to comfort the boy: a kind word here, a reassuring nod there perhaps while passing along a corridor.

One afternoon – according to the mother's missive – the scholastic had driven him out to the village in the school carriage where they had refreshed themselves with lemon cordial and iced buns before trotting the horse and carriage on to the Wicklow foothills. At first the boy was calm. Then he began to make timid enquiries. Should they not return to school? Would he not be punished for this extended breaking of bounds? He should really be at study now, he reminded the scholastic. On the near side of Ballymore Eustace, where the road rose deeper into the hills, the scholastic had pulled up the reins so that the carriage rolled onto a grassy verge. Tomás Tutty froze on his seat, then resisted the hot, protuberant lips, fought against a torrent of words he did not understand and then the explosions of threat and menace. There was a fierce tussle across the front of the carriage. Only Tutty's left hook spared him as he reshaped the scholastic's nose for the rest of his life.

On returning to Clongowes the boy was released, the scholastic mumbling excuses about having picked him up on his way to the village. The state of his face he accounted for with a story of a near collision with an escaped bull on the road which caused him to pull up hard and fall from his carriage seat. At the time Tutty said nothing and took his punishment for breaking bounds.

Months later, whether through guilt or fear of consequences, the scholastic confessed the afternoon's events to Gerard Hubbard in the school chapel. He was sweating and tearful on the other side of the iron grid. Before the young man opened his mouth Hubbard pitied him, recognising a troubled soul. Had they not all been troubled at some time, he and his kind? It came as a shock then when the scholastic's confession concurred fully with what was described in the mother's letter, which Fr O'Connor had, years later, shown him in strictest confidence, although both accounts lacked accurate words of description. But he knew that what had transpired was unspeakable.

Honouring the seal of the confessional he had never since spoken of it, silenced by the darkness in his midst. Was he horrified? He raked his brain again. Yes, of course, he'd been horrified. Tutty had nearly been destroyed.

The truth was: the Order knew. They always knew something. He always knew something. But there was no speech for such knowledge. They knew about the bullyings and they must also have known about the scholastic's unhealthy inclinations. Being a meticulous priest, fidelity to the rule of Church being uppermost in his mind, Fr Hubbard could never have betrayed what was confided to him. He had known a great deal, he realised, but had secreted it away for many decades.

Yet the Provincial, a mere boy companion to Tutty at the time, could surely know nothing of the intricacies of the episode. It was not possible. And the scholastic had long left the Order, thank God, having gone instead, Hubbard had later heard from the Rector, as a missionary to equatorial Africa, the Belgian Congo. As far as Fr Hubbard knew, the man was still there, asylumed, undiscovered. Another thought struck him. *Still unhealthy.* He shuddered. Oh, the knowledge he had possessed down the years. It was almost as bad as being part of it. He thought of the laiety, the justice-seeking new women who would soon be voting for the first time, insistent reporters, most of them with their snouts firmly in the trough of an unseemly, cruel past, supping by the hour on evidence and more evidence which they dared not splash across any but the gutter publications, not all of it accurate either. But of course people possessed an appetite for salacious living.

They revelled in it. They now possessed the power. Looking across the Clongowes playing fields from his high window he had a terrifying vision of how the new power and knowledge were going to raze the many-mansioned heaven-on-earth, eventually emptying the Vatican. He imagined the Holy See in the future. An historical footnote for a new world in which only the finite mattered.

So he was to be punished, was he? He lay down on his bed and shut his eyes. His train of thought was ridiculous, laughable even. Even if he knew, Mark Fitzmaurice couldn't possibly give any weight to a sad incident from one boy's past and connect it with him. In fact, he couldn't have known even the half of it. It was absurd. It was his own guilt rising in the face of his perfectly reasonable reaction to the Provincial's decision. Which was to send him to the equivalent of the polar wastes, which would not draw on the things he knew and loved but would demand that he change everything about his daily life for the sake of the needs of some of the city's greatest failures.

Jesus in Heaven, he thought, sweating lightly. It was to be Temple Gardens for him, a complete uprooting into a crowded and dark city parish house at the ranker end of a street off Gardiner Street where he would be surrounded by all the people in his care. Throngs of mothers with drunken men and too many children they had had carelessly; the poorer classes had never had much self-control, especially where drink was involved. Then there were the gamblers, the wife-beaters, the beggars who would come calling to the parish house. There he was supposed to flourish, or to cause others to flourish presumably, but without sports fields, cross-country runs, without his boys and no prospect of having either of these to work with.

He detested poverty's diminishment of the human spirit. In poverty nothing happened but the learning, at best, of a distorted humility which came from having always to be grateful for the mushroom-like conditions with which one was surrounded: darkness and manure, to be specific. He recalled how the people had behaved in the wake of the business at the GPO two years before. There was nothing but raiding and pillaging of shops by the lower orders. Admittedly the people had nothing so in a way it was understandable. If a nation could not feed and care for its own then perhaps its own had to look out for themselves.

Fr Hubbard found himself ruminating on as he swung his legs over the side of the bed and stood up to pace the bedroom once again: could he turn fate to destiny? He doubted it. In any case fate was a little too Calvinist and he had always rejected it. Destiny was another matter, a little more Catholic in that it allowed for second thoughts and changes of mind that created different outcomes.

Visions assailed him of the kind of person he was *not*, of the priest who arrived into a community to be gently grafted on until trust was gained, before embarking on a transformative programme of – what? Moral talks in the parish hall? Lofty discussions on the evils of alcohol? Choir and organ thumping for groups of women and men in need of diversion? Sports? *Women's* gatherings? He shivered. Yet there was worse, something he had been spared for years. He shivered again. Confessions for the adult masses.

Whatever it was he was not that kind of person. He did not want to have to listen to the weekly maunderings of people who believed they had sinned when in fact they had not sinned at all. How would he teach such people that the Kingdom of God was not an account system that operated from a Debit and Credit ledger? Did he believe in sin? The Jews did not, though whether that was to their advantage remained an open question. To think he would now have to go to the underbelly of Dublin and somehow adjust!

This was not the journey he had ever imagined. Not at this stage in his life. It was all very well to bring boys to Clongowes where the school could work with them, turning them into men of substance, but it was quite another for him to be fired into the searing ovens of new Ireland with its turbulent, agitating women and its divided loyalties. The new nation was not yet properly born.

Another concern struck him. When he departed the school would his name eventually appear on the roll of honour on the Ratio Studiorum Gallery wall? That at least he could hope for. That he might not be completely erased from the school's history. He had breathed life into those boys. He had moulded them from their barely-created twelve-year-old crassness, selected and set them off on the sporting adventures of their youth during which they became men and thought like men and enjoyed being men among men.

What would he do without the boys? At the thought he shut his eyes and bunched his fists tightly against them, screwing them hard until all was darkness within. Within six short months he would have to forsake his green turret room with its view of the playing fields, the sumptuous horse chestnut tree, the weeping ash from which blackbirds flew every spring in full-throated volleys of time and season. Opening them again he blinked and his glance fell on the playing fields beyond the window. The branches of a bare cherry tree swayed in the wind. For a moment watching it distracted him, and his thoughts became less clear, the arguments blurring.

To his surprise he realised he was now hungry enough to face lunch. He checked his fob watch. There was still time to eat. Fr Lenehan would be there and a few of the other priests, though not all he calculated. At least Lenehan was quiet and mathematical, not given to small-talk once he had aired his few small obsessions. He glanced around the room, regarded himself quickly in a small, cracked mirror, then paused before a photograph of Clongowes in the winter of 1910. It had been taken by the photographer father of a third-year boy and drew him back to the time when the whole country had been visited, it seemed, by the Snow Queen herself and shivered in minus eighteen temperatures for weeks at a stretch. Carriage marks on the frozen avenue drew the eye straight down almost to vanishing point except that the eye arrived at the Castle itself, white-turreted and roofed, locked mysteriously behind a fretwork of beeches and limes, themselves so white as to look like breath, exhaling towards the old building, stretching with frozen fingerlets towards that imagined vanishing point.

But they were all in the process of vanishing, he thought, closing the door to his quarters smartly and turning towards the staircase. There was nothing for it but to accept. As he left his room he thought of lisping Tomás Tutty, perfect in all respects save for his speech, and the Westmeath mother who had arrived, like a bronze-winged Archangel, to her son's aid. He wondered where Tutty was now. Which side had he been on in recent years? Had he gone to Europe to fight, he wondered, or would he have lived respectably at home, in the legal profession perhaps? Would he have been sympathetic to the leaders of the rebellion, watching as the new nation convulsed into uncertain life?

That afternoon as he went to lunch his companions were already speaking of Christmas. Fr Lenehan was planning Midnight Mass while Fr O'Connor was disputing the choice of Christmas carols proposed by the choirmaster. It was far too early for such things, he thought disconsolately, it was only the first week in December, so he made little attempt to contribute to the conversation. It being a Monday, cook had roasted pork and potatoes with cabbage and carrots. There was stewed apples and cream for dessert, something he enjoyed.

Fr Hubbard sighed as he poured himself a small glass of Bordeaux. He took a generous sip, let it sit in his mouth a moment before swallowing carefully. It warmed him, already he could feel its curative strength easing him. Again he recalled the scholastic, as far as he knew still in the Congo, in the deep, unsettling heat of the Equator. He wondered what quiet havoc this man might have wreacked in the intervening years if his nature had risen to become the black tree already throwing forth shoots during his time at Clongowes. It would be a perplexing new year. He did not know whether he had the stomach for diplomatic investigation nor did he know just what he was capable of. In his experience diplomacy was usually the portal to something less truthful than its opposite. Even with the change underway and his coming life in the city he realised with growing clarity that he had uncovered a new mission, one he must urgently pursue in the name of justice.

As he left the table he wondered about a church in which there might be people such as Tutty's mother.

THE MOSS-PICKER

Gradually the sound penetrated the homes on both sides of Hill Street. The Misses Coffey darted out like wrens to hover on their doorstep. The spinster Campbell daughter stood frowning and Florence Duffy drew her sons – who had been playing on the street – close to her skirt as the hullabaloo built. Town smells drifted on the air: smoke from coal fires up and down Glasloch Street, stew from the Misses Coffey's kitchen, visceral smells from the abattoir farther down the hill which had had a delivery of cattle that morning and the usual warm, gluey fug that wafted from the blacksmith's forge on Park Street that was neither pleasant nor unpleasant.

Being absorbed by Dr Henry Nixon's housekeeper Clara, nobody noticed these odours. She faced the front of the Nixon household, her body rigid and prancing, arms in fists as she screeched her worst. To the onlookers' surprise nobody emerged from the towering white house to call her in or to comfort her and no window was drawn up. Nor did anybody watch anxiously from the parapet behind which the Nixons often enjoyed an evening cocktail on their continental-style garden roof above the town with its carefully-tended and sheltered palm trees. In winter when all other trees in the town were bare, the Nixon palms could sometimes be seen fluttering bravely above the parapet. Now the house was silent, the windows blinkered even in broad daylight, the pale grey front door closed to the world. Each time Clara paused to catch her breath and begin again the town fell silent. The listeners realised that normal business had ceased since everybody else was also on full alert to her words and their import.

'Henry Nixon,' she shouted, 'how could you do this to me?'

Again she flung pebbles from the margins of the road right at the Nixon front door where they landed with a rude spatter. Indeed, the blacksmith observed, Clara Macken's right hand and arm were stronger than they looked. She began to weep and weaken, every so often stooping to gather a small fistful of stones in one fist but flinging them with less viciousness than before.

'How could you? How could you?' she implored. All ears sharpened as the housekeeper's litany of complaints peppered the air with words such as 'disgrace', 'indecent' and 'immodest'. The sense of shock deepened and some sympathy too, especially from Florence Duffy whose eldest son had been born two months prematurely after a hurried wedding, and who had been subjected to all kinds of speculation both during her pregnancy, when it was commented on that she was obviously going to have a rather large child, and afterwards when knowing smiles accompanied the many gifts for her first born.

In a final attempt to assuage her rage Clara lifted a small rock from the neighbouring garden which fronted the house of the newly-arrived solicitor and fired it hard, directing it not at the Nixon front door but at one of the blank windows which betrayed nothing except for half-drawn blinds and a sumptuous maidenhair fern.

'Did I misunderstand you?' she sobbed, 'You *promised* me!' With these words, the rock struck the long window of the generous reception room in which the Nixons liked to entertain friends and acquaintances, smashing it. The crash of glass seemed to extend in time, slow, glue-like and full of echoes, when in reality it had smashed within a space of three seconds. To those listening it continued to echo with all the drama of a piece of theatre from one of the travelling troupes that had recently visited the town.

People began to withdraw then. For the most part they pitied her for her sobbing and the word 'promise', which held a particular, quavering hopelessness. The blacksmith shook his head and withdrew into the forge, nodding at a farmer who had just arrived with a blinkered dray horse.

Behind their door and in their small parlour the Misses Coffey listened on, each reading the other one's reaction on her powdered face.

'Oh Louisa, poor Miss Macken sounds very unhappy,' whispered one sister.

'Eliza, that is to put it too kindly,' replied Louisa with vinegar in her voice. She shook her head. 'That man!' she added with an annoyed tut. Louisa had once been briefly courted by Henry Nixon, who, for a reason never apparent to her, had not remained true but had begun to dally with Diana Montgomery of Bessboro Hall whom he went on to marry. Although the Misses Coffey were charitable, each recognised that Henry had again behaved true to his nature like the cad he was and, even worse, that he had insulted not only his wife Diana and her entire family at Bessboro but had despoiled a mere girl – the housekeeper! – and now the whole town was buzzing like a wasp's nest with the knowledge.

'How atrocious for Diana,' Eliza said with a little puff.

'It's dire,' Louisa replied with less conviction as she smoothed an antimacassar along the back of her fireside chair, saving her sympathies instead for Clara Macken, whom everybody in town knew would pay severely for the crime of having a romantic heart and being easily lead by manly sweet talk. She wondered if there was anything they could do to help her then decided there was not. After all what did they know of the case beyond what they were now surmising?

Louisa again glanced out her front window. The Coffey house lay at the turn of Hill Street and Mill Street, right on a rounded corner, so the two sisters had the advantage of being able to see up the hill if they peered to the left and down the hill right as far as Church Square if their eyes turned to the right. It was most advantageous, they often agreed, the slight curve on the front of the house affording them an almost global scrutiny of goings-on around the town.

Of course Dr Nixon had decided to build a high wall across the road from his own garden, the effect of which was to partly obscure the view up towards Hill Street. Its purpose, the Coffey sisters had no doubt, was to spare the Nixons the sight of hordes of townspeople straggling and nudging along with their snuffling and sometimes bedraggled children. The Nixons were known for their high style and a propensity for elegant holidays in Italy, especially along the shores of Lake Garda. Diana Nixon herself bought all her costumes either in Switzers of Dublin or else she ordered directly from Selfridges of London.

Gradually the sounds of the town resumed and Clara was left to her own devices. She did not expect anybody to come to her side, to speak to her or to walk with her. There was scarcely a pause in the morning's activities even if she had just given great scandal. She moved away from Hill Street and made her way towards Lake View where she lived with her parents and five brothers. She was the second eldest, her sister Peggy having departed for Dublin the previous year. She felt sick, aware that she could not yet impart her news, aware too that it would not be long before word of her display would find its way to her mother and father. She was sick from her pregnancy and more sickened yet by the thought of what she could possibly say. Her life was destroyed, she knew that for certain. For who would have her now and who would employ her except perhaps the nuns? They took in many kinds of girls, from fallen ones like her, to the poor scraps who were bewildered and not right in the head.

She thought back to the months at the Nixons when she had worked hard to keep their home in the manner in which Mrs Nixon required. Everything must be spick and span, her mistress would announce at least weekly, running somewhat thick fingers along a banister or a windowledge, checking for dust. At first she had not minded Mrs Nixon in the least. If anything, apart from her exhortations about housekeeping, she kept her distance and allowed Clara to proceed with her work. Because the Nixons had no children their laundry was light. Clean sheets weekly, clean underthings daily, fourteen shirts weekly because Dr Nixon sometimes changed his shirt halfway through the day, especially if he had been treating an infectious patient. Fourteen pairs of socks also. Wool in winter, silk in summer. His long johns, Clara had noted on more than one occasion, were not attractive items but he swore by them and declared that he could not have survived so many visits to the country in his new automobile were it not for the addition of long johns beneath his britches and a woollen blanket over his knees. She disliked ironing long johns and pyjama bottoms on account of the loose opening at the front of both. When she saw these she would try to quell the images which rose in her mind and the immodest possibilities that such loose-fronted garments suggested.

How he had sweet talked her! And what care she had taken when ironing his shirts. They were no trouble to her as she pushed the heavy iron up and along the sleeves, nudging the point right into every crinkle and tuck so as to create a clear, creaseless garment that held the warmth of the iron for some moments after she had carefully folded it.

She remembered exactly when the affair had begun. She would not have called it an affair. Only women in big cities and faraway places had affairs. She did not have a term for it but she knew that she had loved him. One late afternoon he had come up behind her as she was ironing. He had stood there a moment. When she turned she met his eyes, which were regarding her fondly, what she would have called affectionately. Even with the small distance between them – he did not touch her – she could smell him, the whole, delicious, slightly-scented odour of a clean man.

'You are most industrious,' he remarked in a low voice.

At this she blushed, although she was already pink in the face from her work.

'It is my job.'

'You do it so willingly. So well.'

She smiled and averted her eyes. 'I'd better be getting back to it so,' she told him.

Things happened very quickly then. She could hear Mrs Nixon's footstep on the landing upstairs, the tap-tapping of her heels as she stepped along down the passageway that led to her bedroom. Mr Nixon reached and placed his hand on her left forearm as if to halt her. He took a step towards her. Clara, paralysed yet wanting something to happen, did not move her body, instead tilting her face slightly upwards and to the side. Then his lips. The pressure of them, soft, soft on her hot little cheek. She closed her eyes and almost gasped.

Then he was gone from the kitchen, with a whisper she could not understand. Or was it perhaps an exclamation?

Clara had held on to her secret for one week after her public display in front of the Nixon's house. Her father had been labouring three miles away at the Rossmore estate, where he had also bedded during the harvest and so – inexplicably to Clara – the news did not reach him at all. It fell to her mother to tell him. Clara's mother had wept when she heard of the upset. It was all so public. Why, she berated Clara, did she have to behave in that way? Clara knew that the question covered both issues, her present situation as well as her indecorous display out on the public street. But her mother went on, inconsolable and raging. Hadn't she told her about the need for modesty at all times? Hadn't she told her to say three Hail Marys for purity? But she had had this feeling in her body, between her legs, that had come the moment Mr Nixon had kissed her and although she had struggled for a while it was beyond her to help herself or resist for long.

'*Dearest Peggy,*' she wrote on the evening the nuns took her in.

> *I have just arrived in the convent, where Sr Regina tells me I am to stay for the next months until I have made arrangements for myself after the birth. You will now know what has hapened and I am most sorry, dear Sr, for any embarasment. I can hardly hold this pen to write, and but for the fact that Mother has already writen to you herself I would scarcely be able to find any words at all. Daddy was so angry that he himself gathered my clothes – all the wrong ones I might add so that nothing matches – into a sac and tossed it onto the street. Mammy did not wish this, of course, but he forced her back into the house despite her begging for mercy. She actually begged him, dear Peggy, to have mercy on me. Can you imagine it? Even though she is disgrased, embarased beyond words, her mother's love did not dessert her and even though he overpowered her with his unreesonable will and his body and in the end threw me out I will never forget Mammy's kindness.*

Clara put down her pen and stretched her fingers to relieve the tension in them. This was her first letter to anybody and it was a long one. A heavy tear bounced down one side of her cheek as she thought about this. What a shame that letters often brought bad news. She regarded the cell-like room in which the nuns had put her.

It was very white and clean with the narrowest little bed she had ever seen. Her ill-assorted garments dangled from a long rail which had been fixed between the chimney breast and the mostly bare shelves on which lay a bible and three books, one of them by Mrs Henry Woods. She had heard of this writer. Mammy enjoyed her novels.

Her eye wandered to the window. She was not quite ready to continue this letter with its request. Outside lay the long stretch to the Bog of Allen. Tufts of rushes thrust upwards on the soggier stretches near the convent grounds. Bulrushes prodded. Even the low, uneven grass was full of spikes, which was how her mind felt just then. A heron crawked somewhere in the distance. It was a place for shy creatures and secrets, she thought.

Even the convent was a secret, beyond the ken of Edenmore, the nearest town in the midlands. She had glimpsed the main street as the omnibus rattled through. It was long, not as busy as her own town, and wide, the widest street she had ever seen. Horses and carts were parked at odd angles and the smell of animal urine came through the open window near her head, acrid and steamy. It did not, to her relief, make her feel ill. There was a YMCA hall, she noticed, much smaller than the one at home and, of course, a church. Beside it stood a square limestone priest's house with many chimneys. She counted eight decorated ochre chimney pots and marvelled at the number of fires that could be lit in one large house for one person if he so wished. But soon the omnibus lumbered on into the countryside and she got off as instructed in Sr Regina's letter just after they passed the second crossroads. As she hauled her suitcase out the conductor took a look at her.

'Away with you so,' he murmured with a nod and a hint of a smile.

'Thank you,' she replied automatically, brushing her coat down and adjusting her hat.

Two nuns waited in an open carriage. One of them introduced herself as Sr Regina, the other as Sr Aloysius, who was sturdy and dark-browed. She did not smile as she took Clara's valise and placed it at the back of the carriage.

'We'll be off so,' Sr Aloysius said, 'it's not far.'

She took the reins and whistled and the horse moved off at a bright clip.

Ten minutes later Sr Aloysius relaxed the reins and the horse turned in at a brisker trot through a large, laurel-hung entrance.

'He knows he's going home,' Sr Aloysius chuckled to Sr Regina.

'Where he'll get his belly filled,' the other nun replied.

A set of black cast iron gates were pushed open and the carriage proceeded along the gravelled avenue which curved several times before arriving at the convent.

The main house was four storeys tall and very grey. At the sight of it Clara felt herself sink into a state of fear, her homesickness deepening as she looked out at the land around it which was silent, empty and brown with the bog. She did not think she would survive. How could she live in a place like this so far from the lovely little hills around her own town with its woods and streams? Automatically, and as so many times recently, she swallowed hard to suppress the tears that began to soak her eyes. Sr Regina glanced at her.

'We'll show you to your room. You'll meet the other girls later. At teatime.'

The work in the convent was such that it became a world of its own, protected from prying eyes. There was prayer and work and sleep and not much in between, even if the nuns were not unkind. Largely invisible to the world its secrets were so very different from the feeble secrets of the rest of ordinary society, Clara reflected miserably.

Reluctantly she tilted her head to the page again, read what she had already written and dipped her pen in the porcelain inkwell.

So my situation is truly dredful. I am sick not just in the mornings but all day even as I work scrubbing the floors and polishing the halls and emptying the slops from the kitchen. Oh the smell of all that makes me feel very very poorly. I imagine also that insence from the chapel seeps into the stones around the convent. I smell it everywhere, there is no excape from it. Sometimes I see no possable point in my life. You are the only person I can confide such feelings to. Nobody here has the slightest simpathy for me, well that is not quite true as Sr Regina is very nice and even if I am feeling sorry for myself I think I have the reason to. Henry – Mr Nixon – ignored me from the moment he made me his, you know what I mean, I think it was as if all the affection shown to me was gone and he became so cold I thought at first my imagination was fooling me. But no, once he had sweet talked me into loving him he turned away as if I was nothing, as if I was a rat from the canal.

You are very wise Peggy and you know plenty about the world so perhaps you will not be surprised at this. How I wish you were at home and not in Dublin with young Mrs Wheeler and how I wish you had stayed here and not grown so upset by young Arthur Duffy's death in Flanders. I should not scold you for this of course. You were very great with the Duffy's and they with you. So I am being most selfish in this wish. But Peggy, I am imploring you. Do you think that Mrs Wheeler might have need of a girl like me, a willing, hard-working girl? This, I mean after I have had my child. Perhaps I can find a wee house in the city, do you think? Do you know of any such places? I could be happy and caring with this small babby, you know that, even though nobody would want to know me I think, not being respectable any more. But I am good with my hands and could take in work, mending and fixing. I could work very hard to provide for my child.

Dear Peggy, you know that I am axsing you to think about this. I hope you are not shocked. You are older than me and there is nobody else. Please ask your Mrs Wheeler for advise. You also told me that Mrs Wheeler's mother is a modern woman who helps other women. Please see if she could help me. Or perhaps you know of somebody who needs a good girl even if she is in the family way and with no husband at her back.

I pray for you every day, that your work is not too hard, not that you were ever afeard of work but you know what I mean. And I pray that

you are happy in the city and that its ways are not too awful. Sometimes we hear stories of life in Dublin and how dirty it is and how anything could happen on the streets when the Peelers turn on the people. I think I am afraid of the people there even before I get there! But please help me if you can. I am desperit.
Your loving sister,
Clara.
PS My waist has not yet begun to thiken so I do not look as if I am carying a babby. I think I could work for quite a long time before anyone would notice. Tell your lady that I look most respectible and that I am clean and do not smell, and honest.'

She re-read the letter, checking the words, knowing she had misspelt many of them but hoping nonetheless that Peggy would understand her dilemma. Sometimes it was not enough to write things down, there were ways of showing the recipient how one felt and underlining was one of the ways she had devised for this purpose.

It seemed like months, but it was not. It was a mere month and two days before she got used to convent living. Work cleared her head and her heart. Four weeks of labour and two extra days. Thirty in all. She calculated them on her fingers, watching the first four weeks of seven days sweep by and then the final two, during which she grew a little calmer. A few of the nuns prevented her from undertaking the heaviest work. Sr Regina, who had collected her from the bus stop outside the town on her first day, liked to mind the girls through their pregnancies. She was a bony woman with a strong Tipperary accent who had never forgotten her own large and rumbumtious family reared in the shadow of the Galtee mountains. In the convent in the midlands she too pined within the flat and bog-brown landscape and this loneliness found an outlet in spontaneous sympathy for the girls who had found themselves in their uncelebrated plight. Part of her remembered the welcome each new arrival had got in Galteebeg, as the farm was called, and the excitement when her Papa would bring the new little one downstairs for the other children to inspect. The baby would be freshly swaddled, smelling sweet and damp and so fresh from the womb that nine-year old Regina, whose real name was Mary, once shrieked in excitement that the baby smelt like a warm scone out of the oven.

Once, when Clara vomited into one of the rose beds behind the Novitiate on her return from hanging up a bulky basketful of sheets, Sr Regina insisted on bringing her to the nuns' kitchen, sat her down beside a warm range which oozed waves of such heat she could have fallen into a slumber there and then.

'Sure you poor girl,' she whispered, handing her a mug of tea. 'And is your stomach sick every day?' she enquired, rubbing Clara's shoulder.

At such sympathy tears leaked out of Clara's eyes and she stifled a sob.

'Now now, dear,' the old nun went on, kneeling down in front of her. 'You just take a few sups, it'll put the rosies back in your cheeks! You must stay strong for the sake of your babby.'

'I know, Sister.'

'Try to offer it all up for our own poor Irish heroes who were shot in Dublin eighteen months ago on account of their activities. Think of their families, Clara! Offer it all up for them.'

Clara tried to sip the tea but had not the heart to tell Sr Regina that the executed men in Dublin were now long dead and therefore out of pain. Furthermore the tea was so scalding hot and had so little milk in it that she could scarcely let it touch her tongue. Nor had she the heart to respond to her by saying that surely it didn't matter whether she was strong or weak because in the end the baby would be taken from her. Instead she smiled wanly at the nun who allowed her to sit until she was recovered. She realised she would quite like to have stayed with the nuns but the truth was that after the birth she would remain for three months only before giving up her child to some respectable couple. The only girls who were permitted to remain in the convent were already orphaned girls without babies or girls who were a bit backward and had no other place to go. But she would have to go somewhere, she knew that.

She befriended another girl in the same condition as herself whose similar cell-like room lay opposite her own on the third-floor convent corridor. Helen was from Waterford and came from a family of coal merchants. She was not proud or snobbish, Clara quickly realised, as the pair of them worked together in the laundry or in the kitchen. They both preferred the kitchen, and gradually, owing to a mutual skill for bread baking and pastry making, found themselves working there oftener over the months. Helen's baby was expected a month before Clara's, inasmuch as she could guess correctly. She never spoke about the father of the child and at the slightest mention of such matters went silent. She was four years younger than Clara who formed the impression that Helen had been forced into her condition; that it had not been a question of falling for a man the way Clara did, even if he had taken advantage of her too. And although she had told Helen about Mr Henry Nixon she did not elaborate too much on what her feelings for him had once been. Feelings, if she allowed them, could wander into the kind of terrain that unsettled her for days.

In one such fantasy she imagined Henry arriving in his automobile, having searched the length and breadth of the country for her. She saw him arriving in a desperate state in this little narrative and told her that his wife and children had been murdered in their house while he had been out in the country attending to a patient. He was distraught but looked to her – and only to her – for comfort. Head in hands, he told her that it was she, and only she, he had ever loved. Living without her was an impossibility. He must have her, he must bring her and their unborn child away from this place and would build a new life for them both, with a fine house, a view of the sea and a beautiful sandy beach below. They would leave the pain of the past behind for good.

But this was quite inhuman, she realised. How could she wish the death of the very people Henry was attached to, even if his love of them was questionable and of poor quality? In the end she learned to banish such fantasies and got on with the day-to day world, expecting nothing, but enjoying her conversations with Helen.

Helen, being younger, was slightly giddy. As Clara watched her friend's belly enlarge and yet watched Helen jump and leap at some comic notion, it often cheered her up. Helen was like a gambolling child and she saw the funny side of things, provided she was not thinking about her pregnancy. She liked riddles and jokes and to recount her schooldays with the Ursuline nuns in Waterford. Clara, who had been taught by the St Louis nuns in her home town, felt a certain competitive envy when Helen came out with a few Greek and Latin words. She tried to counter this by trawling up one or two German words which she remembered from her one year in secondary school before her father had decided that the education of girls was wasteful and that they could not afford to have her not working.

The words she remembered were the ones the other girls used to laugh at: *oder* and *Fahrt*, for example, because of the way they sounded. But then she also said the word *Liebe* and at this they both smiled. Even Helen, despite her situation, was not immune to *Liebe* and would very much like to find some of it, wherever it could be found.

'Isn't it well for the ones who got to finish school?' Helen said one day as her fingers broke down the butter, sugar and flour into a crumbly mix for pastry.

Clara, sweeping the floor of the nuns' kitchen, grunted as she bent to pick up a piece of paper – her belly was growing very large – and agreed.

'But then what'll they do with the learnin' when they get married? All those ones get married and have childer.'

'I suppose they can teach them a bit. And they can talk as if they know something when they go out into society,' Helen replied.

Clara turned towards her and leaned on the sweeping brush as she caught her breath. To her it was not so simple. She told Helen how Henry Nixon's wife Diana had been to university and studied science but Clara had never observed anything about Mrs Nixon that made her think she was educated. She was interested mostly in her attire, she told Helen, who listened with wide and interested eyes. Oh yes and she was mad about planning visits to London or Dublin or Italy, Clara went on, encouraged. She also regarded local life with some reservation and mixed only with two or three other families. The right kind of families, ones with money but who did not read books, Clara suspected. Diana Nixon occasionally rode out with them or attended winter parties on the estates outside the town. Sometimes in summer she would judge a gymkhana and meet English and French visitors who came to her parents' home behind the high stone walls of Bessboro every July to ride and to fish. But she had no real interest in the local library or the schools and although the librarian had invited her onto the Committee for the Promotion of Excellence in Reading she had written him a polite note thanking him for his kindness but explaining that she was often absent from the town and therefore would not be much use. Clara knew this because she had seen Mrs Nixon dashing off the letter as she herself was dusting the morning room. Her quick eyes had caught the phrase 'absent from town' and 'not much use'. Clara had then had to post the letter even though the library was only fifty steps down the street.

As she was in the middle of telling this story the diminutive nun in charge of the kitchen, Sr Thomasina, hurried in with a bucketful of winter turnip and some kale which she then placed in the large Belfast sink.

'Wasn't she the right lazy trollop!' Helen exclaimed quietly, ignoring her, balling the pastry in one fist and slamming it down efficiently onto a floured board.

Sr Thomasina's head snapped around and she glared at Helen. 'That's enough of that language, Miss!'

'Sorry, Sister,' Helen said meekly.

'Lazy? No, she was not lazy,' Clara replied thoughtfully as if the nun were not present. 'She simply couldn't be bothered. That's the kind of woman she was. She found plenty to be energetic about when it suited her. Just not books and just not being too friendly with the townspeople.'

How different Diana Nixon was from her own mother! Clara's mother read books and she was a poor woman with little education but the works of Sir Walter Scott and Charles Dickens had taught her many things and ideas. She often wished her father had had a tendency to read books as well but he was barely literate so she could hardly blame him because it was difficult to master the words. Indeed her own book knowledge was not so good and she was, she knew, a poor speller.

'Oh I can spell!' Helen said, pleased with herself. She was now rolling out the pastry. 'I was the best speller in my class all through school.'

'Now you're bragging,' Clara teased, a little jealous.

'Yes,' Sr Thomasina interjected, 'And there's no place for pride in the Kingdom of Heaven. Remember that, girls.'

'I'm not braggin', Sister! 'Tis only the truth.'

'Well be careful, girl. Pride comes before a fall for all of us.'

The girls got on with their work in silence. Sr Thomasina began to peel the skin off the turnips and then set to rinsing the leaves of curly kale and setting them in a separate ceramic bowl. The turnips she placed on the wooden draining board to cut and slice into small pieces. Every so often she helped herself to one, blessing herself before she did so and chewing carefully because some of her back teeth were missing.

As Helen eased the rounds of smooth pastry onto the waiting platters, heaped the sliced apples and added sugar and cloves, Clara polished the range and then set about heating a huge steel pot of water. It would be needed for scalding the thick hairs off the flesh of the freshly-slaughtered pig which one of the farm nuns had just that day finished off herself. It was a self-sufficient institution and the nuns rarely met with either priest or bishop beyond their obvious daily presence for the offering of the Mass and the hearing of Confession each Saturday evening.

'It's a strange thing,' Clara said dreamily, watching the steam rise from the pot, 'how we're doing all the things a wife would be doing. Look at us. Like women in any kitchen with babies in our two bellies. Except we're not in our own kitchens and we have no men.'

'Enough of that talk now,' Sr Thomasina interrupted again, gruffly but kindly.

But as it happened Helen had no wish to pursue the conversation and looked uncomprehendingly at Clara. She did not enjoy being reminded of her situation. She resented the turning and movement of the baby in her womb because it kept her awake at night and she was afraid of what would emerge from her body when her time to deliver the child eventually came.

'We have no men and thanks be to Jesus for that,' she said quickly, brushing down the front of her apron before removing it.

'Girls, would ye stop profaning!' Sr Thomasina cried out, rinsing her hands and shaking her head in despair. 'I don't know what's to become of the pair of ye if ye insist on such open conversations. Ye'll only upset yourselves even more.'

'Ah, Sister, don't mind us,' Clara said. 'We know a lot about the truth now so we might as well tell it to one another. And the truth is that since the war some women have no man in the kitchen or in the bed. So maybe we're not as badly off as we think we are, Sister.'

'I suppose it's good to be optimistic,' the little nun sighed.

Christmas in the convent was not an unhappy affair, although Clara wept in secret in her room thinking of Mammy and Daddy and wondering if they missed her. A tree would have been brought in from Rossmore Park and Mammy and the little ones would have decorated it with twists of coloured paper and pine cones strung gaily along the branches. There was even tinsel and a red and gold star for the top of the tree. Surely Mammy missed her!

Sr Regina and Sr Aloysius were brisk and cheerful throughout the season and although the weather that year was particularly cruel, the harsh cold kept illness at bay and none of the girls caught colds or flu. Outside the kitchen the holly hedge was peppered with red berries and Sr Regina cut small branches to bring inside and arrange throughout the convent. There was a Christmas tree in the long parquet-tiled hall which led to the chapel and the girls were encouraged to decorate it. There were fifteen of them and they set to piling it with ornaments and coloured hoops of paper. Sr Regina insisted on climbing the stepladder to place the Christmas angel on the topmost spear of the *Tannenbaum*, as she called it, using a German word which Clara also remembered from her year in secondary school. The nun was afraid that one of the pregnant girls would tumble off the ladder and land herself in serious trouble.

Thinking of the *Tannenbaum* reminded Clara that she wished she had not had to curtail her education or been asked to. She had quite enjoyed German and Latin and the Christmas choir in which the first years had sung sweetly *Oh Tannenbaum, oh Tannenbaum, wie grün sind Deine Blätter* ... But with the arrival of a second baby brother – she remembered her mother's long moans from the bedroom as the midwife stayed through the labour – every farthing mattered.

Despite the gaiety of dressing the tree Midnight Mass was another matter. Many of the girls wept because it was impossible not to feel lonely when the nuns' voices rose through the notes and words of *Silent Night*, their simple harmonies carried through the scented-candle air towards the deep claret and azure of the stained-glass windows behind the altar. Clara had never felt so far, far away from love and ease in her whole life. This was it, she thought. She would always be alone, unhappy and unloved. Nobody would ever care for her and she would not even have the care of her own child to tend to the wound of her broken heart.

But it passed. Christmas dinner the next day was quite merry and she began to feel more at ease again. For a while it seemed as if the girls forgot their station, their position and what lay ahead of them. Jokes were told, there was nudging and giggling, so much so that Sr Regina announced with a twinkle in her eye that they were like a crowd of giddy-goats. Her situation would improve, Clara told herself again and again. She was not a girl for sitting back and allowing life to do things to her. She would do something, would mend life to her own size and fitting.

That determined thought pursued her into the New Year and, as the birth approached, she felt strength building within.

One night she heard a commotion in the corridor outside her room, hurried footsteps and whispers, then the slam of a door. It was ten o'clock and most of the girls were in their rooms or in the recreation room listening to the gramophone which was permitted for an hour a day. The babies were normally delivered by the nuns themselves in the convent. The local doctor was called only in a case of emergency and afterwards to check that the new mother was in good health.

Curious, she opened her door a crack. Sr Aloysius was hurrying along the corridor with a bucket of steaming water, a heap of towels on one arm. As she had suspected there was a crisis, and in Helen's room. Despite the prohibition on walking around the corridors after ten o'clock at night, Clara darted out and stood squarely in front of Sr Aloysius, whose face was bathed in a light sheen of perspiration.

'What's wrong with Helen, Sister?'

'Oh, child, she's gone into labour and it's not coming easy for her. She's so small, d'ye see? I knew when I saw those little feet of hers, only a size two, I just knew it wouldn't come right for her. Small feet, small pelvis, d'ye see? The doctor's on his way. Now go back to your room and pray.' Sr Aloysius looked seriously at her. 'Will you do that for me? Say your prayers. It might be the only thing to help us. It's too late to move her from her room and there is a lot of bleeding.'

Clara bit her lip and returned to her room. She stood for a while with her back against the door, breathing in and out slowly, trying to calm herself. She had forgotten the thing about small feet and had always thought it an old wives' tale, a superstition. But perhaps it was true. Helen's size two feet must mean she was very very small in the lower department and that there was not enough space for the baby's head to come through.

Trembling, she went over to her narrow bed, let herself fall on her knees and began to pray. Prayer, although it had never changed anything for her – she had prayed very hard that her monthlies would return after she began to suspect she was pregnant with Henry Nixon's child – sometimes brought a certain calmness. She had never given up the habit and found it helped to clear her head when she was very weary. But as for asking for things through prayer? She almost scoffed out loud. She would never ask for anything because that was insane and people who thought prayer could change something as immutable as a physical emergency or the weather or coming death were living in a fairyland of their own creation. Nonetheless she picked up her rosary from beneath her bolster and fingered it for some moments before commencing a decade of the Hail Marys her mother had so often advised her to say. For purity. At that thought she smiled. Now she must pray for poor Helen. She sensed the Angel of Death hovering somewhere in the air around them as she knelt for an hour at least, trying not to hear Helen's cries and the encouraging voices of Sr Aloysius and the doctor with his deeper timbre, and then more cries which rose from time to time to a terrible scream. It sounded like torture. Yes, her friend was undergoing a torture such as she could only imagine. *God help her, God help her*, she whispered miserably as she prayed on. From time to time she thought what a strange sacrifice it was to be born a girl at all for it seemed as if so many of her sex gave their lives in unnecessary ways or because they had fallen accidentally in the direction of what was unnecessary. It made her nervous for the birth of her own child.

Ten hours after she had begun to pray, not even before the first crack of dawn was showing on the flat horizon, Clara stirred in her bed, having scarcely slept. A door had opened and there was a new urgency to the mixture of murmuring voices and silence that accompanied it. She threw back the blankets, sprang out of bed and opened her door. As she did so she felt her baby turn in her womb, disturbed by her sudden movements. Sr Regina was holding a small, tightly-wrapped form close to her own chest. Even at a glance Clara knew the child was dead. She saw the tiny face, its pallor and waxiness, the little purpled lips. The nun was crying softly. The doctor was speaking to Sr Aloysius; he looked very grave. But worst of all was the sight of Helen, her eyes half-open, stretched out on a trolley that had been brought by the ambulance men in Tullamore, where there was a hospital.

'Helen!' Clara cried out, springing towards her.

But the girl did not recognise her. Her skin on her face was puffy and grey, streaked with blood and sweat, her lips cracked and at the corners of her mouth pools of saliva had caked and settled. Even her fingernails, Clara noticed, were embedded with what looked like dried blood. Helen groaned softly and turned away expressionless. She looked as if she wanted to die.

The nuns were upset by this turn of events. It was not a common thing and Sr Aloysius, when speaking to the doctor, reminded him that there had been no infant death during her years as Mother Superior, that is, she emphasised, for the past ten years. He was not accusing her, but Sr Aloysius, disturbed by what she had witnessed as the young girl pushed to the edge of her life to give birth to a child whose head was too large for the passage to the outside world, felt as if some blame was due to her for not being able to do more. By the time the doctor arrived it had been too late to attempt a Caesarean section or at least that was what he had adamantly informed her.

Three weeks later, Sr Regina called Clara to her office. She had been sweeping the long hall that led to the convent chapel and which had to be burnished and gleaming at all times. By now her stomach was large and firm. She followed the nun slowly, wondering about the official nature of the request.

It was a letter. Sr Regina held it up for her to see. It had been opened, Clara noticed, her eye lighting on the serrated envelope and slightly torn stamp. And it was from Peggy, she noted, recognising her elder sister's rounded script.

'Sr Aloysius forgot to deliver this to you, my dear. I fear its contents may be out of date,' she began.

'Forgot? *Forgot*?' Clara whispered.

She reached forward and tried not to rip the envelope from the nun's hand. She was raging. To think the letter – a letter to her from her elder sister – had been read by a stranger, by someone who had no business knowing her business!

'Thank you, Sister,' she said in a small, tight voice, unable to articulate her rage.

'You may sit and read it, if you wish.' Sr Regina beckoned towards a low green armchair. 'Take a little rest for yourself.'

Clara paused. For a moment she was going to. That chair looked so enticing, so comfortable compared to the hard upright chair in her room, that to sink back and just read a letter seemed like an excellent idea. But no; whatever news was in the letter, and which Sr Aloysius had long ago read and digested anyway, could wait until she was in the privacy of her own room again.

'No thank you, Sister. I'll read it later,' she replied, before slipping the envelope into the pocket of her pinafore.

The nun frowned, as if rebuffed. 'Well I do hope it's nothing important. I am sorry that you did not receive the letter on time.'

'Ah sure,' Clara sighed, turning to leave, 'there's never any news that's so exciting it can't wait a bit. Even so, Sister Regina, it was my news to receive and not Sister Aloysius's and you'd be doing me a great favour if you would tell her that from me.'

'That's enough out of you, madam!' the nun suddenly flared up. 'Do you realise how fortunate you are to be here with us? To be looked after in this style and safety, when nobody else would have you?'

Clara turned in the doorway and looked back over her shoulder. So even Sr Regina was so infected with this disease, this way of looking at girls like her, that she would come out with words like that.

'It's true, Sister. Nobody else would have me. I am grateful.'

Her heart pumped strongly as she made her way back down the corridor, kicking an empty bucket that stood outside the nuns' parlour. It made a satisfying clatter. Someone else could finish the hallway. She had a letter to read. She made her way to her room and closed the door firmly behind her. Throwing herself onto her narrow bed, she whipped the letter from the envelope.

Dublin, February 5th, 1919
Dear Clara,
I know of course about your situation because Mammy wrote to me immediately. I am sorry it has taken so long to write back to you. I wanted to think about what would be best and I am kept very busy here at the Wheeler residence where the Mrs, a lively lady I have to say, keeps us all busy. I am fond of her though and she is unlike any lady I have ever met. I hope you can forgive the silence.
It will be impossible for you to find work in the city with a baby. A girl with a child will get no respect or only if she is fortunate enough to meet decent people like the Wheelers perhaps. Well, I mean Mrs Wheeler and her mother Mrs Ward, if I'm to speak the truth! Mr Wheeler is a conundrum and quite moody at times since they returned from foreign parts although he dotes on the Mrs after a style. But that subject is not for this letter but for the time when I get to see you, dear Clara. I do not know if I can help you but my

intention is to get a day and a night off and travel to Edenmore to see you. I will take the train to Newbridge and the omnibus from there. Do the nuns allow visitors? I will not be able to come for another while as there are all kinds of uproars in this house at the moment as the Mrs settles back into life in Ireland. I know you will probably have your baby before I get to see you. The Mrs has persuaded Himself to allow her to attend the university – no less! – to study for a degree so there is a mood of great nervousness as she makes arrangements to ensure that the children are looked after at all times. He is afraid she will become infected by the Gaelic League and such people as go to the university. Himself is such a traditional man he does not understand that they can breathe and eat and play without their mother being there every moment of the day.

And now, dear Clara, I hope you are feeling better, and not so sick. It is hard enough being pregnant without being sick too, I imagine. And I sincerely hope the sisters are kind and that you are not working too hard. A woman carrying a child needs more rest than usual so I hope that is permitted …

At this last comment, Clara smiled. Rest! There was little rest in the convent, except on Saturday evenings and Sunday afternoons, because the girls were kept busy cleaning, mending, doing the laundry, ironing, cooking and, where possible, some gardening. The hours of rest were intended for reading uplifting literature – the novels of Mrs Henry Woods, poems by Rudyard Kipling, Charles Dickens's *David Copperfield* and *Nicholas Nickleby* and their own Lady Augusta Gregory whose retelling of the Irish legends interested some of the girls. There were also several thick and colourfully-illustrated Bibles for those who wished to read them.

Try not to worry for now. I will see you when I can and time will surely fly and soon you will have your baby. I hope it is a safe delivery and I hope for the child's sake that it is born a boy. You will understand why.
Your loving sister,
Peggy X X X

The three kisses made Clara weep softly for a few moments. She placed the letter on top of the *prie-dieu* and anchored the pages with the small metal crucifix that stood in each of the girls' rooms. It was a long time since anybody had either kissed or hugged her. When poor Helen was there they had hugged in their girlish way and that was consoling. But nobody else had so much as touched her flesh in a gesture of kindness. So to see these written kisses on the page practically overwhelmed her. Hot, self-pitying tears bounced down her cheeks and she swung her feet off the bed so that she could sit up again and blow her nose. She wished the baby would come soon but had no exact clue as to when that would be. Any day now, she sometimes thought, any day now.

Her labour, when it came, was so unnoticeable that she was working right up to the hour when she delivered her child. There had been a few pains, little niggles in her belly throughout the day. In the kitchen, as she once again made brown bread, she noticed a dull ache in her lower back. Just as she pushed the final trays of bread into the oven, pulling away sharply from the oozing waves of heat that assaulted her face, her waters broke. For a moment she thought she had wet herself and gazed, terrified and panicked, at the sweet-smelling pool that spread around her feet.

Before she knew it, Sr Thomasina was at her elbow, steadying her.

'Your time has come,' she whispered, 'I'll call Sister Apollinaris.'

Clara did not know that there was such a thing as an easy delivery, especially a first delivery. She remembered her mother's deep animal groans when the last of her brothers was born, only two years before. It was a sound that had frightened her, and her father not even in the house because the labour had come unexpectedly, leaving her to calm the children while the midwife encouraged her mother upstairs.

By the time Sr Apollinaris arrived to her room she was on the narrow bed, underthings removed, lying on the hessian sack, the child's head was already nudging into view.

'Sister!' she called, reaching out to her with one hand. 'I want to push but I'm afraid of making a mess ...'

'That's all right, child. The head has crowned. You can push. Push very hard now,' the nun replied, her hands lightly tracing the baby's shape on Clara's abdomen.

In no time at all the child slipped out, warm and steaming with womb fluids. She held her son to her chest and inhaled him, the sweetness of him, the pink and whiteness of his creased little monkey face. A son, it crossed her mind with relief, would have some chance.

Peggy arrived to see her when the baby – Patrick Joseph – was five days old. She too had made her way to the convent in the old bus out of Edenmore, had got out at the specified stop and briskly walked the two miles to the convent. Sr Regina called Clara from her room, saying she had a visitor. She seemed excited, Clara thought, and very much on her best behaviour. When she saw Peggy below in the hallway, standing beneath a statue of the Little Flower, she knew why. For a moment she paused, startled almost into non-recognition at the sight of her sister who looked glossy, healthy and quite fashionable. She could be mistaken for a lady from the upper reaches of society, Clara noted, or at least one would not identify her as having come from the lower end. Patrick Joseph was asleep in his iron cot so she hurried down the curving staircase towards Peggy, arms outstretched, not taking the final three steps in one quick jump as she would normally have done but treading quite carefully before landing in her arms. As she did so her breasts released a few droplets of milk which they seemed to do at any and every opportunity but particularly when she was emotionally moved.

'You came!' she laughed, checking the front of her dress hastily, 'And just when I'd given up.'

Peggy was wearing a dark purple costume tucked and trimmed to suit her figure. Lightly she threw back the folds of a fine wool coat with black velvet buttons all the way down and smiled at Clara. A net veil quivered over her forehead from the front of her black velvet hat.

'I said I'd come.'

Sr Regina, who had taken in the stylish appearance of Clara's elder sister, watched the unfolding reunion with inquisitive eyes, then withdrew and left them to talk. Peggy, eager to see the new baby, followed her sister up the three flights of staircase and they turned left down the long corridor which led to her room. Clara opened the door quietly and Peggy stepped in. She looked around, frowning as she took in her surroundings.

'So this is where they've had you? All these months?'

Clara shrugged. 'It's not so bad. I got used to it.'

But Peggy was distracted by Patrick Joseph who stirred in his cot and turned so that his face was visible. She leaned in over him and peered at the infant, absorbing everything about him from the wide forehead to the little sift of hair on his bald and pulsating skull to the daintiest nose she had ever seen and the clearly-marked lips with their tuck of a chin beneath. His eyelashes quivered in sleep and his face squeezed itself into a shape that suggested he was about to cry but in the end it relaxed again and the eyelids were still and sealed to the world.

'You are so fortunate,' Peggy breathed out, straightening up. 'Something I'd never have thought I'd say.'

'Do you think so? Do you really think so? Because he's the loveliest, best baby alive. I want to keep him. I told you that already.'

Peggy sat on the edge of the narrow bed. 'You know you can't.'

'I can if I want to.'

'How can you keep him? You have no money.'

'I know, I know. But I'm thinking a lot and –'

Peggy sighed. Thinking a lot wasn't going to solve the situation and it was up to her, now, to persuade Clara to relinquish the child and have him adopted by people who really could care for him. Even women like Mrs Wheeler in Dublin couldn't do much without money, at least a husband's money, behind them.

'It's a question of what you want for him, Clara. What do you want for him?'

Clara did not reply. The words were easy. 'The best and only the best' sat on her tongue but she did not utter them. Because Peggy's response, were she to say them, was all too obvious. How could she give him the best and only the best, she would surely say?

In the end Peggy did not press her further. She did not want to fight with her younger sister who was so alone. Innocent too. Had she any idea of what lay ahead? And yet, Peggy thought, lifting the baby from the cot and rocking him carefully, she had done this one great thing. Nobody thought anything of the great thing. Nobody valued it. But she, Peggy, did. She felt a pang of something bordering on envy in her heart as she beheld the perfect child. This was something she had never known, although she had a few men friends. The nearest thing to maternal satisfaction came through the Wheeler children where she was entrusted with a great deal of their care while Mrs Wheeler attended university lectures on Earlsfort Terrace and Mr Wheeler worked. They were like her own flesh, though she rarely admitted it to herself and she loved them while acknowledging that they never were and never would be hers. They would grow up and away into their own society. If she was lucky the Wheelers might keep her on into old age. At this stage she did not expect to meet any man who would suit her, somebody kind who would also enable her to choose whether or not to work with the Wheelers. And although she loved the Wheelers she had not had any choice. She had merely been fortunate to meet such a good family.

They each played with the baby, cuddling him, turning his tiny hands, bringing him to the window when his eyes eventually opened, showing him the world and the sun and the distant brown bog. In the distance a curlew went *pee-iu, pee-iu,* and then gave an even longer *pee-iu* in its solitary terrain. Already Clara was an expert at changing Patrick Joseph's nappy and happily demonstrated her new skills before her sister.

'He's perfect, isn't he?' she said.

'He is,' Peggy acknowledged. 'Quite perfect.'

'So, the next thing is for me to recover and in a few weeks get out of this place. With Patrick Joseph,' she said firmly.

'God help you, yes, with Patrick Joseph.'

Then Peggy informed her that she had no offer of a position in Dublin but she did have something in mind. She had enquired of Mrs Wheeler, who had mentioned the matter to her mother Mrs Ward. Mrs Ward, she told Clara, was one of those women who had fought for female emancipation.

'Female *what*?' Clara asked, puzzled.

'Votes for women,' Peggy explained. 'And all her work is for the relief of women in difficulty. She believes in a woman's right to shape her own destiny and she says that only comes when women earn a fair wage for fair labour.'

Clara didn't quite see what relevance this had to her, but she did need a job. Mrs Wheeler's mother had written several letters on her account to see what the chances were of Clara availing of work anywhere in Ireland.

'You have a chance of work but it's not in Dublin.'

'Where is it?'

'It's not so far from here. I wonder that the nuns haven't mentioned it.'

'What kind of work?'

'Moss.'

Clara stared at Peggy as if she had lost her reason. 'Moss?' she repeated uncomprehendingly.

'Picking sphagnum moss for bandages. It's part of the war effort even though the war is over. The bandages are still in demand all over Europe.' Peggy's eyes lit up suddenly. 'Would you believe it, Clara, that our Irish moss was being collected and sent to Dublin and then made into antiseptic bandages for the poor fellows on the Front? It's better than cotton and the army hospitals were running out of cotton bandages anyway, but they say it's being put to great use as a surgical dressing.'

'Irish moss? Imagine ...' Clara replied slowly, still absorbing what Peggy was saying. It was hard to imagine anything Irish being very much use any place outside of Ireland. She peered out of the window wonderingly and across at the lip of brown bog on the horizon.

'Moss is even better than cotton and the men's wounds were unimaginable. Awful suppurating wounds!' Peggy added in a grim voice.

The nuns would not have thought to mention such work to her, Clara mused, because they fully expected that she would be relinquishing her child and returning to her home town to resume life there as if it had never been interrupted. She smiled at the thought of herself returning to her own hearth and perhaps getting another housekeeping position in the town as a young single woman. But there would always be a dark stain on her, like an invisible, watery but unpleasant ink, which everyone would see and never forget. No matter how respectable she became she would have this part of her life hanging over her and nobody to share the sadness of her loss. But she was not going to suffer the loss of Patrick Joseph. She was not going to endure that for the sake of holding a respectable position in a place where nobody very much cared for her or her life unless she obeyed what strictures their little society required. She often thought of home and it brought a pang to her heart because she loved it, even the town and many of the townspeople, none of whom had ever treated her harshly even after the uproar on the street outside Henry Nixon's home. She pondered the possibility of actually returning where her mother would surely allow her to bring Patrick Joseph.

Surely she would be charmed and delighted by the little fellow? But then she considered her father who might not be so pleased after all if the manner in which he had ejected her from her own bed all those months ago was anything to go by, telling her to gather her things and throwing her out onto the street against her mother's wishes. No, she thought, she could never return home. At the thoughts of home she thought inevitably of Henry Nixon. She could never return there to the possibility of bumping into him on the street perhaps or seeing him and his wife sail out into a summer evening in their automobile. To think that she now had *his* beautiful boy in her care and he would never, ever, know his son. It saddened her because she believed that Patrick Joseph should have a father who would acknowledge him and hold him and take him as his own. But that, she knew, was a fairy dream, one that most people would laugh at, even if kindly.

She kissed Peggy on the cheek and smelt her sweet scent – *Midnight Lily*, it was called, Peggy said – then waved her away down the long avenue to the outside world where she would once again meet an omnibus which would carry her across the undulating bog roads to Edenmore and onwards to the Newbridge train. They had formed a plan and Peggy assured her that she would help her see it through.

'You are mad though, you realise that, don't you?' Peggy said, touching her cheek fondly.

'Does determination make me mad?' Clara whispered.

A week later she felt already quite recovered from the birth. Strength poured back into her and not even feeding the baby sapped her. Sr Thomasina plied her with warm milk and malt in the kitchen every evening before bedtime and a thick slice of wheaten loaf with butter and jam on the grounds that she must keep up her strength. Otherwise the life of the convent carried on as usual. There were usually one or two nursing girls and there was always a new girl arriving in a state of shame and some despair who had to adjust to the routines of the convent. And there were the ones who were abundantly pregnant and waiting for their babies to be delivered.

The day that Peggy announced to Sr Aloysius that she intended not to have her baby adopted, the old nun stared at her, horrified.

'Surely you cannot be thinking this way, Clara. Have you lost your reason?'

'No, Sister, I have taken this decision in the full of my health. I do not want to lose little Patrick Joseph.'

Aloysius stood up from the deep mahogany desk which separated her from Clara, moved her chair and turned to the long window for a moment. Clara followed her gaze. Swirls and furls of grey cloud approached from the west. Parts of the sky were still blue and this blue was reflected in some of the puddles and ponds beyond the convent fields.

'Your child would be reared lovingly by a good Catholic family,' the nun said thoughtfully. 'He would be reared in the true Faith. He would be given every opportunity as he grows. Every opportunity ...'

She turned back to Clara, her eyes angry and concerned at once.

'I will have to call in Fr Pierce if you intend to follow this foolish notion. It's not only foolish but downright dangerous.'

Clara stirred and looked at her, puzzled. 'How is it dangerous, Sister?'

'A lone girl bringing up a baby? Don't you realise how hard your life will be?'

'Yes, Sister, I do. But I have hope too that things will improve. That I can work.'

The nun gazed at her unsparingly. 'That you can *work*. How ridiculous!' she spat.

'Please, Sister, do not call in Fr Pierce. There is nothing he can say to change my mind. I am satisfied that I know what is best.'

'Well, I am not!' Sr Aloysius raised her voice and thumped the desk with her large fist, before sitting down heavily once again. Immediately she bent and opened a drawer to her left, withdrawing a file. From this she withdrew some papers. She thrust them towards Clara.

'You must fill these in. You can write, I take it?'

'Of course I can write,' Clara replied, stung by the nun's impertinence. She lifted the documents and read them quickly. If she signed them she would forego all rights to her child. 'But I can't fill those in. My baby is staying with me.'

They sat for some half hour and argued. Clara knew that once she signed anything she would forfeit all rights to hold on to her child. At one point the nun, in exasperation, opened another drawer and withdrew a bottle of lavender water and a small white handkerchief. Hurriedly she spilt a few droplets onto the fabric then dabbed her forehead and temples.

'Now see what you are driving me to, child. You have given me such a headache I can hardly think straight.'

'I'm very sorry for that, Sister. I didn't mean to,' Clara said meekly.

'Please leave and return to your room. Fr Pierce will stay for breakfast after Mass tomorrow morning. He will have to speak to you then,' Sr Aloysius sniffed. 'It is for the best. You must let him advise you.'

Clara thought of Fr Pierce with his broad pink face and smiling careful eyes. When he sneezed he could be heard all over the convent. The girls used to laugh as he sneezed, calling him a braying donkey. But that was men, Clara thought. They could do what they liked even with the sounds their bodies made which everybody was supposed to think nothing of but which were sometimes an embarrassment to polite society.

That night she swaddled Patrick Joseph, then wrapped him again in two warm shawls, one of them brought by Peggy on the day of her visit. Then she slipped down the long corridor to the curving back staircase which would bring her below. She passed a framed picture of the Sacred Heart, with its all-seeing eyes but did not care whether he was watching her or not. The little red votive lamp below the image flickered as she passed. In the kitchen she eyed the range which had been tamped down but through which the glow of red cinders seeped at the grate. How comfortable it would be to stay, even for another while, she thought in a moment's sentiment, thinking of the days with Sr Thomasina and Sr Regina and even of Sr Apollinaris who had given her such strength as she gave birth and had made her feel proud of herself, if only briefly. And she remembered young Helen who had had such a dreadful time of it but who, she hoped, was restored by her family in Waterford despite what had occurred at the time of her child's birth. She checked her suitcase again: clothing and nappies for the baby, bottles of water, no worries about the child's nutrition since her breasts were plump with milk and could satisfy him easily. It was a question of walking all the way to Edenmore and of taking the train to the next town where Peggy had arranged accommodation for her and Patrick Joseph with a contact of Mrs Wheeler's mother who was also involved in the alleviation of human suffering for both men and women.

It was a dark night with only a quarter waxing moon to partially light the way as she headed along the road. She had to be careful not to trip and there were puddles and undulations everywhere as the road sagged where it crossed the bog. To her left and right were the hopeless whin-bushes, spiky and bare in the winter night, and the stripped birches and ash trees bent by the persistent westerly wind which moaned across the flattest part of Ireland.

The child barely stirred but by the time she arrived in Edenmore at six o'clock the next morning she was exhausted, sweating and hungry and he was crying and gurning for his feed. She made her way to the station, safe in the knowledge that nobody at the convent would yet be aware of her absconding in the night, found the Ladies rooms opened but as yet empty and positioned herself behind a heavy locked door in one of the closets. There she fed her baby, surrounded by the soft hiss of the sanitary waterworks trickling into cisterns above her head, knees spread for comfort as she sat on the wooden lavatory seat, leaning back against the water pipe for support. The child took his fill and she relaxed as he relaxed. When he had finished, his red lips wet, a droplet of milk hovering gluey-white in the corner of his mouth, she waited a while, recovering, and drank a great deal of the water she had brought and a few cuts of bread from Sr Thomasina's kitchen. Then she changed the baby, balancing him on her spread knees and in the heft of her skirt. By the time she unlocked the lavatory door, other female passengers were arriving to use the closets. She emerged and tried to look composed, crossed to the mirror above the sinks and made a tranquil show of checking her appearance which was the one thing all women without exception did upon emerging from a closet. But the women only glanced at her and looked away not seeing anything unusual in the sight of a woman carrying a sleeping, healthy child against her chest and one small valise swinging from her fingers.

On the train she grew nervous. She took out the scrap of lined jotter paper on which Peggy had written an address and a name. *Mrs Maud Conroy, 4 Slí na Sí*, it read. The arrangement was to be a temporary one of five months and Clara would give half of her wages to Mrs Conroy who would care for her baby while Clara was out on the bog.

The train pulled in slowly with a long screech and the intensity of its arrival momentarily distracted her. There was the steam and a clutch of men and women waiting to board and travel onwards to Newbridge she guessed or even to Dublin. She disembarked and stood for a moment, gathering herself. She did not know how this arrangement with Mrs Conroy could work, given that she was breast-feeding. She scrutinised Peggy's directions on another sheet of jotting paper and left the station grounds, turning left past a long trough of water for the horses reined in by their owners who sat perched on top of carts and carriages. There was one automobile into which an elegant woman disappeared, only to be driven away. A few winter pansies squinted wanly at the low sky from within two earthen pots and convolvulus and ivies twisted within the bare hedges. After half a mile she crossed the main street. Her pace slowed as she made her way along a narrow footpath beneath stalls of winter vegetables to which the clay still clung – turnips, parsnips, carrots, cabbages and beets – and past one tea shop. She stared in. Clara was dying for a cup of tea and perhaps a bun. But again she grew nervous and resisted the urge. The place was full of the women of the town, sipping teas, nibbling on iced buns and, her hungry eye noted, brandy snaps. She could not possibly enter that place and survive their curious eyes.

The dwelling was a high three-storey building of grey brick with a bright green front door, and *Slí na Sí* was a side street that led to the bog and slid downwards into a deep hollow before the road went straight out into the foggy edge of the world. To her surprise there were window boxes crammed with pansies with soft black faces and yellow and purple wings of colour. It looked so gay and bright that her spirits brightened in turn and she lifted the polished door knocker to announce her arrival.

Mrs Maud Conroy was unlike any woman Clara had ever before encountered. Dressed in the very latest ankle-revealing dress, but with sturdy brown shoes, she made her welcome, opening her arms immediately to relieve her of the baby, leading her to her room on the first floor. It was one of the quietest, she explained, being at the back of the property with a view down the hill to the creamery. It was almost ten o'clock and a trail of horses or donkeys and carts loaded with milk churns waited in a line until the milk could be taken in at a platform. She watched a man on the platform chatting to a farmer as he hoisted his churn. They seemed to be engaged in easy conversation and the farmer laughed at something the other man said. But, as Maud Conroy explained, the room was quiet and Clara would never hear a word from any conversation down the hill, only the occasional clang of metal as the churns landed on the platform.

Within a week her milk had dried up. It was all for the best, Mrs Conroy said, that she should mind the child while Clara worked.

'Don't get dolled up in fancy shoes and fancy clothes,' she warned, 'because the work is hard.'

'I don't have any fancy clothes,' Clara replied waspishly. She was tired and advice of any kind was not welcome.

At first she wept bitterly in bed. Her breasts were hard and engorged with milk and the pain grew for a few days, so much so that even the feel of her chemise brushing lightly across her chest was enough to cause her pain when she dressed in the mornings. But eventually it subsided, like a river drying up, all her goodness and wetness, her nourishment sinking back into her own body. It was for the best and she knew it.

Each day she was collected in an old army cart with a canvas roof and a small churn of fresh milk attached to one side. The driver, whose name was Dillon, never spoke. She did not know his first name. It seemed nobody else did either. All that was known about him was that he had seen action in Europe in early 1916 and that while crossing the Mediterranean on a troopship his vessel was torpedoed and sunk. More than a year later he occasionally offered scraps of his story as he muttered erratically to people about being adrift on a lifeboat. When he was rescued he was taken to Alexandria where he spent two months recuperating from head wounds. Now a metal plate covered part of his brain, Mrs Conroy explained, and he never removed his hat because his skin had never been properly replaced. He was still in shock and would probably remain that way. Clara observed his pale skin, with its first lines of care etched prematurely between his eyebrows and on his cheeks, imagining him lost at sea and then alone in a strange country with nobody by his side to pray for him in his own faith. He would have been a dashing-looking fellow in his uniform, she thought, and perhaps if he were dressed differently and had his hair cut he still would be. But then there was the problem with the head, the exposed metal plate beneath his brown hat. She did not know if she could bear to see that.

Dillon's silence suited Clara who needed time to settle and consider her own position. She did not feel calm or happy at first when so much that was uncertain lay ahead. Dillon also collected three other workers for the day. There was a widow whose husband had died at the Somme, and who rarely spoke either. Some days she wept silently and her tears were like a steady leakage from her eyes and down the sides of her nose. There was also a disgraced priest who had left his religious order and was trying to fit into normal society again far away from his own community. Beside him in the cart there usually sat a deaf-mute boy of sixteen.

In a way she found it easier to travel the few miles out to the bog with such people. At first she felt fearful leaving Patrick Joseph behind her. It was the first separation and it seemed unbearable, but gradually she grew accustomed to it. She felt safe with her companions in the cart. She never felt as if they thought badly of her. Indeed they had such problems of their own that for the first time she felt gratitude. She was in the full of her health with a beautiful baby boy and her whole life ahead of her. The widow, she thought, might never recover from her husband's death and as for the priest – there was no place for *him*, and all he had apparently done was to change his mind about his vocation some years after ordination. Only the deaf mute boy might be safe, she thought. Or perhaps not. Sometimes when a person couldn't speak bad things happened to them. And even though she could speak there were things she would never be able to utter for the rest of her life, or if so, only to a limited few. It was far, far too hard to discover the right words. If only they had the right words, she would think. Then everybody could explain their own sadness and perhaps it could be understood. They were all, in a way, silent people.

The bog was peppered with people bending down, picking the sphagnum. Like coloured specks the labouring bodies stretched out a long way from where she was working during her first week, backs stooped over the plants as they moved along slowly, picking, picking. She was given a basket by the overseer, a man from Antrim who also showed her exactly what the moss looked like and how not to remove anything other than moss.

'We don't want grass or anythin' like that,' he said gruffly. 'Just moss.'

'Just moss,' she echoed, nodding.

The ground was very wet that first day. Clara worked alongside the widow and the deaf mute boy. The disgraced priest was brought over to a different area by the overseer who then returned for some time to observe Clara and her companions as they worked. The wind whipped across the plains bringing drenching rains in its wake. Soon the water was trickling steadily from the heavy India-rubber rainwear fastened around Clara's neck and draped down along her back. It caught the back of her dress and then seeped into her stockings and the backs of her worn boots. With every step her foot sank into the springily wet ground with its brilliant green mosses on top. Because the soles of her old boots were made of leather they quickly absorbed the moisture from the ground and in no time her feet ached with icy wetness.

The days passed like ponderous blades descending on the hours, chopping the minutes in little pieces so that not for one moment did she sense she was getting anywhere. But where could she get to? Filling the baskets with sphagnum was no problem but wondering where it would all lead was another matter and she felt stagnant. Yet even in grim weather the green around her was vivid and inviting and she imagined what a soft bed it would make in a dry summer if one had the opportunity to sleep out beneath the stars. Then she scolded herself for being so romantic. Sleeping beneath the stars. That would never happen to her, she thought regretfully, either alone or in the company of someone else. She had long given up on romance and even Patrick Joseph's startling resemblance to his father – something she occasionally thought might change Henry Nixon's attitude were he to be presented with his own flesh and blood – did not deter her from the belief that she must carry on alone. She suddenly felt sorry for herself as the skies darkened even more and the rain poured steadily down with no sign of abating.

It took almost a day to fill even one basket because the workers had to pack the moss down tightly so it took many hours for it to rise anywhere near the top. At one o'clock they stopped for a break. Another cart arrived with huge pots of boiled potatoes that were still quite warm particularly if you managed to get the ones from the middle of the pot and not the top. There was fresh milk and fresh buttermilk. Clara loved buttermilk and gulped it down, enjoying the tang that was the only thing that really sated her thirst.

'Keep goin', keep goin',' the overseer urged them back to work. 'There are sick men yet all over the world and we're playin' our wee part.'

Although her back ached by evening time, as the weeks passed she began to think that he was right. They were playing their part. Even if there had been chaos in Dublin when the rebels had fought three years earlier, even if they had been scandalously executed by the British, there were the tail ends of this other greater war. They must still remember the thousands of Irishmen who went to Flanders and to France for the sake of defending what was right. One day to her surprise the widow spoke while they were gobbling down their dinner.

'Nobody in Ireland has the slightest idea of what it was like for the men abroad,' she said in an expressionless voice.

Clara did not speak. She waited.

'Their wounds were so terrible that ordinary bandages were not adequate,' the widow explained. 'Their flesh, rotting and running, their burns terrible. Men squealing like stuck pigs with the unmerciful pain. I know that from my – my dead husband's letters. It makes me proud to work here. I imagine that some man who will be healed by our bandages is some woman's sweetheart ... even if the war is past.'

'There's that at least,' Clara replied, uncertain of what to say.

It seemed to encourage the widow. She rooted in one of her pockets and withdrew an envelope which she proceeded to open. 'To think they started out so well,' the woman said softly, holding two sheets of paper in her hand. 'They were so cheerful too. Would you like to hear what he wrote? This was at the beginning, you know.'

Clara nodded. It appeared she had no other choice but she felt nervous of this sudden moment of revelation from a woman who had scarcely opened her mouth in the time she had known her.

'My darling', she read,

I received your welcomed letter and was glad to see by it you are well and in good health even if missing me. I am feeling well with the exception of my loneliness for you, my sweet. You will be surprised to read that we have landed in Leamington Spa since Jan and expect to leave on the 20th. There is some rumour that we don't leave until the end of the month. It may be sooner or later and it don't matter as all is ready. I thought we may miss action until the weather would be better. It is horrid to be in trenches in cold weather not mind wet – however pot luck the most of the lads here have seen Indian action and other places. There is nothing like having the hard nut, the green un is easier cracked – we are having a glorious time here even if we miss our beloveds, much as I hate to tell you such things but it is the truth. The finest place I have seen, yes, splendid people, no barracks here, all billeted in houses – both public and private. I am in a large confectioners, something to make you smile, my dear, knowing my love of sweet things, so plenty jam tarts and ice cream. We have theatres by the dozen – picture gallery even, we partake of some Spa – well when we feel that way. This is the famous Leamington Spa here. We can get to a hall every night, open from 2 to 10. You can get a cup of tea and about 4 ozs curren cake for one halfpenny. A thousand and one of such places, we will feel lonesome when we leave. My darling I am sending my old army papers to you for safety, until – that is if – I return. But do not fret, I intend to return and the Hun will not best me. I have no more at present but I remain yours as always. You are in my heart and soul and on my return we will have such times. I am thinking of the family we will have, dearest, and the children that will make us even happier than we are.

Fondly, and adoringly,
Your Jamesie

There was silence when the widow finished. Throughout it all the tone of her voice never once wavered. She read it evenly, then folded up the pages, slipped them into the envelope and concealed it deep in her pocket again.

'Thank you,' Clara whispered, again at a loss. On impulse she reached across and placed her hand on the other woman's. But she shook it away and dipped her head for a moment before looking up and away into the distance.

For the rest of her time on the bogs Clara never heard her speak again but it was enough to make her consider the men who were still in Europe. It was true. None of them could understand because they were not there. All pain was particular to the sufferer no matter where he lived and although people knew that great suffering occurred they could not feel for it unless they were affected by it personally. The widow was affected by it, Clara thought, so her understanding was deeper. It was a way of doing something useful that might help some man just like her dead husband and might ease his misery in some far away hospital.

The baskets of moss were collected at the end of each day and brought to the Grand Canal where they were ferried to Dublin and a depot on Merrion Square. At the depot unpaid women turned the moss into bandages.

My God, Clara thought one day, *my hands are touching materials that will soon touch the burned flesh of people I do not know and will never meet*. And she imagined the places the bandages would travel to, their cleansing mossy contents picked by people like her, ordinary people with ordinary problems, to be sent to places far, far away. France, Belgium, Egypt, even Salonica. Someone had said that the 10th Irish Division had fought in Salonica against the people of the Balkans who were known to fight to the death. After all hadn't the whole war started down there when some madman shot the Archduke on his visit to Sarajevo?

Sometimes it was hard to retain such thoughts of greater good and working for others and selflessly, as hers were so often deflected back to Patrick Joseph who was thriving under the care of Mrs Conroy. When she arrived home in the cart late each evening in the early spring of 1919 she began to feel more hopeful. The infant would yelp and gurgle with delight when he saw his mother, wriggling in Mrs Conroy's arms, his plump arms extended towards her. Despite herself she felt a little spark of jealousy towards Mrs Conroy who was getting so much time with her son when she had only the nights. Even so, she consoled herself, it was Clara he slept with and Clara he played with until he dozed off.

During the next two months Dillon began to speak more directly to her on the drive out to the bog. At first it was just an occasional remark about the weather. Or he would ask her if she had remembered to bring her warmest garments because the day was to be bitterly cold.

One Monday she arrived with a head cold and sat snuffling at the front of the cart, her nose red and running.

'That weather doesn't help anyone that's sick,' he muttered gruffly, looking straight ahead with the reins slack in his hands. The two horses pulling the cart were unhurried, despite the rain.

'And these dames aren't too keen to be away from the stable,' he added, jerking his head in their direction.

'Who'd blame them?' Clara replied in the silence that followed because it appeared that nobody was prepared to engage Dillon in conversation on the rare occasions when it appeared he had discovered speech.

When they arrived out at the bog Dillon took his time helping Clara carefully down from the cart. He did this with the widow as well but it had struck Clara that for the first time in what seemed like at least a year she felt a kindly hand being placed on her forearm. Just as Henry Nixon had once done, except that Dillon expected nothing of her.

'Go aisy now,' he muttered under his breath. 'The day will be a short one and there's snow on the way,' he added, glancing in the direction of the Slieve Bloom mountains. Curling cobalt clouds were gathering darkly, full of menace.

With snow on the ground the moss could not be picked but Dillon's forecast was wrong. Instead of snow there was a flurry of sleet, which quickly dissolved though not before drenching everybody and making fingers red and stinging.

Now, though, the evenings were grinding forwards and the days were longer. The light held until half past five when a bright, pale blue sky opened up and cloud banks fell gradually away. By the time the widow, the priest, the deaf mute boy and Clara, as well as another four pickers were back in the cart, they were bedraggled. There was no conversation as they eased their backs against the sides of the cart and gazed passively at what remained of the day. Clara wondered how much longer she could keep up this work.

As she stepped down from the cart outside Mrs Conroy's house Dillon gripped her by the wrist and steadied her.

'Go aisy now,' he repeated his morning exhortation with a slight nod of the head.

'I will, Mr Dillon.' Despite her firm intention never again to smile at a man she found herself smiling. He really should remove that hat, she mused as she turned to go into the house. It would end the mystery of the metal plate. At least in her mind it was a mystery, and slightly terrifying the more she thought about it. He should not hide it so carefully. Unlike some of the men she had heard about, his face was unmarked by burns so his personality did not appear to have been erased.

That evening at supper Mrs Conroy handed her a letter then sat by the fire to darn a few stockings. The cinders creaked pleasantly and the room was so warm that, only a moment before, Clara had felt she would swoon into a deep sleep so lovely did it feel after the harsh day outdoors. She glanced down at the letter. It was from Peggy. She fingered the envelope suspiciously before breaking the seal and opening it. There was obviously not much news in this dispatch if this slender envelope was anything to go by.

How wrong she was.

Clara, I have something to tell you ... the letter began abruptly without the usual endearments and absolutely no address or date. She read on quickly through the bare details and stopped chewing her dinner so surprised was she by Peggy's words. There was almost too much to take in as Peggy's rounded, neat script announced the latest in delightful phrases that included *a gentleman friend these past nine months or so ... did not wish to alarm you when I visited you at Edenmore ... and he is in the printing room at the* Irish Times *newspaper with good prospects for advancement as you can imagine ...*

Briefly she was annoyed that Peggy had not confided such essential information to her in Edenmore but on balance she forgave her. It was an uncertain world and so much depended on the delicate handling of certain situations, especially the acquisition of a suitable husband. Oliver, as he was called, had been walking out with her for almost a year. He was everything she had hoped for in a man: *reliable, kind, tall and very handsome. You should see him stride out with his walking stick, brisk and smart as the best of them ...*

'Why Clara, you are flashing colour like a Christmas lantern, one minute pale and the next pink as a trout! Have you received happy news, dear?' Mrs Conroy enquired gently, putting down the stocking she was darning.

Clara turned to her, her eyes bright and excited. 'It's my sister, Peggy. She is to be married. To a man –'

'I trust it is to a man, dear girl – but what splendid news! How lovely for you,' Mrs Conroy gushed, then sat back to hear more, her darning forgotten.

Clara told her that a wedding had been arranged, with a morning Mass at the University Church on St Stephen's Green. It would be followed by a wedding breakfast at Finn's Hotel on 3rd April. All the Wheelers would attend, Peggy had written, so she would have an opportunity to meet Mrs Margaret Wheeler but must not pay too much attention to Charles Wheeler who was always ill-at-ease about something since his return from the Far East although his heart was in the right place and he truly loved his wife. It was she who had insisted that they attend the wedding and was helping Peggy with her trousseau.

The thing I really wanted to tell you, dear Clara, is that Oliver and I (oh, I can hardly believe that I am writing the words 'Oliver and I', and with such assurance!) have bought a small house in Donnybrook which is not very far from the city. That is to say, it is Oliver who has mostly bought it but as I had some savings I was able to help a little. It is really a cottage on a terrace of other cottages with three small bedrooms. The street is quiet and it looks down to Herbert Park and the beautiful trees and gardens and walks. It is unlike other parts of the city and is salubrious. I have told Oliver all about you and he assures me that he will love you almost as much as he loves me and has insisted that – God willing and if you wish this – you and Patrick Joseph come and live with us until you are settled in the city. Mother and Father will not be attending the wedding, alas, as Father will not countenance my marrying someone from the other faith.

Clara could not finish her dinner at all. It did not matter in the least that Oliver was a Protestant. Perhaps it was a good thing, she thought, and might bring an easier life to Peggy. It seemed to her that many Protestants were upright and yet not overly concerned with some of the regulation of faith that the Catholics insisted on. But, more importantly, something had happened. It was so unexpected and just when she had begun to think that she would be picking moss for ever – or doing something out on the bog – because surely the need for bandages would eventually dry up. But it was not to be. Thanks to Peggy, Fate or God or just chance had intervened and she was to go to the city – at last – with her own room in Peggy's own home where she could be safe while she sought work and tried to further her own prospects. Of course – her mind rushed ahead – Peggy would probably want babies (she was not yet too old) so she would be able to help her during those first months.

Thank you, thank you, thank you! she proclaimed to the unknown force, the sheer, unimagined chanciness that was ushering her onwards.

She worked out the rest of the week on the bog. After that she was to travel to Dublin by train where Peggy would meet her and Mrs Wheeler would permit her to stay in Peggy's basement bedroom, with Patrick Joseph, until after the wedding. She would remain there until the happy couple had returned from their honeymoon in Wexford. As she looked out across the wild acres of tufted green and turbulent brown peat and at the bodies of the other moss-pickers she almost pinched herself as she realised that there would be an end to this labour and that those who were here would continue to be here while she was fortunate enough to escape to something better. It was bound to be better.

On Friday, her final day, she told Dillon that she would not be returning. He had continued to conduct himself in a kindly manner during the week, helping her on and off the cart, sometimes insisting that she take an extra potato from the pot, *to build up your strength*, was the way he put it.

Now though, she could not help noticing how his face suddenly changed, that he looked crestfallen.

'It's good news, girl. Good news, isn't it?' he mumbled reluctantly, adjusting his hat slightly.

'Very good news, Mr Dillon,' she replied.

'John,' he said.

'Pardon?'

'John Dillon.'

It was a little late for introductions. As they stood beside the cart she shook his hand as if for the first time. At that moment one of the horses released a loud stream of steaming piss which gurgled and swirled down into the gutter. The priest had averted his head from the couple and the deaf mute boy stared intently at them as if reading their movements and lips. The widow had also averted her head though a rare, secretive smile played at the corners of her mouth.

'Mr Dillon? John?'

She proposed that she write him a letter when she was settled in Dublin. She would like to inform him of her situation. And then – she hesitated – if it suited him perhaps he could reply.

He seemed doubtful. 'Ah, you'll be busy up there in the city. You'll be whirled away and out with some fine chap – you won't have time for letters,' he said softly.

'Leave that to me,' she replied firmly. 'I keep my word.'

'I – I hope so. That is – if you say so,' he said in a low voice.

They nodded at one another as so often before then he hopped up on the front of the cart, flicked the reins lightly and the horses rumbled and clopped off up the street. As she stood in the doorway of Maud Conroy's house she smiled quizzically. It appeared she had formed an understanding with John Dillon. She did not frighten him or make him feel disgust at her condition. He knew what she was and who she was. All this and with so few words passing between them. And for the first time she realised his still-concealed head wound did not frighten her as much as before.

That night she scarcely slept. She held the infant lightly to her chest, relaxing into the deep softness of his breaths, thinking to herself that some things in life were almost unbearably beautiful and that this was one of them. Through the skylight stars edged slowly across the night.

She was really leaving. In the coming years she would ease herself into full womanhood. She would be a real woman whose girlhood would fall far behind although her deepest mind would carry its marks, its lack of charity, its foolishness, for ever. There would be room for her and Patrick Joseph, she was sure of it, room for their dreams in the modern society that was taking shape in the most uncertain ways. She remembered Henry Nixon who was the cause of her fall from grace, his hand on her forearm and his wife Diana's thick dust-questing fingers. She prayed, not for them, but for all the women who might fall within the poisoned circle of his ilk.

Mary O'Donnell is one of Ireland's best-known authors. Her novels are *The Light-Makers, Virgin and the Boy, The Elysium Testament* and *Where They Lie* (New Island, 2014). Her collections of short stories are *Strong Pagans* and *Storm Over Belfast.* As a poet, her collections include the highly-popular *Unlegendary Heroes, Spiderwoman's Third Avenue Rhapsody, The Place of Miracles* and *Those April Fevers.* She was overall winner of the Fish International Short Story Prize in 2010 and the Hungarian edition of her *Selected Poems* received the Irodalmi Jelen Translation Prize (2012). A selection of essays on her work, *Giving Shape to the Moment: the Art of Mary O'Donnell,* has just been published by Peter Lang UK. She lives in County Kildare.

www.maryodonnell.com
Twitter: maryodonnell03